S0-AAC-587

# BLINDSIDED

As soon as Spur saw the riflemen shooting at the rider, he sprinted ten yards to his tiny fortress and bellied down behind the rocks.

At once a rifle slug hit the foot-thick rock in front of his head. Spur felt the boulder bounce back half an inch as it deflected the heavy rifle slug.

Two more rounds sliced through the dug-in bush branches; then there was a silence. Spur pushed the Spencer through the small hole between the rocks and fired twice into the brush near the cottonwood tree. For a moment there was no response; then two more shots jolted into the boulders inside the bushy blind.

Spur moved enough to see through the hole and fired three times again, then paused. He heard a loud wail of pain and anger, then silence. That was followed by the loud voices of an argument. Spur jolted a new deadly messenger through the brush and the argument stopped.

The *Spur* series from *Leisure Books:*

**#41: GOLD LEDGE GOLD DIGGERS**
**#40: TEXAS TRAMP**
**#39: MINETOWN MISTRESS**
**#38: FREE PRESS FILLY**
**#37: MISSOURI MAMA**
**#36: MOUNTAIN MADAM**
**#35: WYOMING WILDCAT**
**#34: DEADRIDGE DOLL**
**#33: LOUISIANA LASS**
**#32: MINER'S MOLL**

LEISURE BOOKS NEW YORK CITY

A LEISURE BOOK®

April 1995

Published by

Dorchester Publishing Co., Inc.
276 Fifth Avenue
New York, NY 10001

If you purchased this book without a cover you should be aware that this book is stolen property. It was reported as "unsold and destroyed" to the publisher and neither the author nor the publisher has received any payment for this "stripped book."

Copyright © 1995 by Chet Cunningham/BookCrafters

All rights reserved. No part of this book may be reproduced or transmitted in any form or by any electronic or mechanical means, including photocopying, recording or by any information storage and retrieval system, without the written permission of the Publisher, except where permitted by law.

The name "Leisure Books" and the stylized "L" with design are trademarks of Dorchester Publishing Co., Inc.

Printed in the United States of America.

# Chapter One

Twin rifle shots blasted into the dusty west Texas afternoon and Judge Roy Bean came down on all four legs of the chair where he had been leaning back on the front porch of his "Law West of the Pecos" wood-framed headquarters. He stared at the Southern Pacific mixed train that had stopped at the Langtry station only moments before.

"What the hell is happening?" the 60-year-old justice of the peace bellowed. He stood and checked the six car train critically but could find nothing amiss. Then the third car back from the Baldwin engine, the Railway Express car, rocked with an explosion and Judge Roy Bean reached for his Winchester repeater.

Across the tracks on the off side of the train from the shack town of Langtry, Texas, two men had just scrambled into the Express car through the blown off sliding side door. Both wore kerchief masks, both left horses tied to the train car's open door.

One man stepped over the unconscious form of the express clerk and stared at the already open safe. He grinned and began pulling everything out of the safe and stowing it in a gunny sack he had brought along. As an afterthought, he picked up a pair of post office mail sacks marked "Registered Mail" and motioned to the other man who peered around the side of the torn open door, a shotgun in his hands.

The scattergun man fired once down the side of the train, waited a minute, then fired again. He reloaded the twin barreled Greener and checked outside. No one showed along that side of the train.

"Now!" he yelled and both men stepped out of the express car into their saddles, pulled the reins free and turned their mounts. The robber's shotgun fired again toward the caboose, and then another shot at the engine, where the engineer already lay dying of a rifle shot.

The shotgunner pushed the Greener into the boot alongside a rifle, balanced the two mail sacks on the saddle in front of him and kicked his bay in the flanks as she surged away from the train and into the Texas flatland and rolling hills to the east. More places to hide in that area.

The first man had tied the gunny sack full of loot onto the horn of his saddle and kicked his roan. Two handgun shots sounded behind him, but he didn't even turn around. He was well out of revolver range and riding like the wind to get out of range of some rifles that someone must be limbering up behind him.

He ducked low over the neck of the horse as

two rifle rounds sped past him. He could hear the whistle in the air as they missed. He kicked his roan again so she galloped at full speed toward the slight rise that would give him protection from rifles at the train. A half minute and six rifle rounds that missed him later, he curved his mount behind the rise of ground and found his partner there waiting for him, grinning like a she-bear with three cubs.

"Gol dang if we didn't do it," he shouted. "We robbed ourselves a damn train. Now let's get the hell out of here and find that creek we picked out so no sonofabitch can track us. Then we can get to the cabin where we can figure out exactly what we got here."

The man was Texas thin, had a well worn gray-dirty low crowned cowboy hat on and when he pulled the kerchief down from his face, he showed a tanned, range wise face with a fist-broken nose, green eyes and three days of black whisker stubble. His eyes danced with excitement that had been too long in coming. For years he had dreamed of becoming a real Wild West desperado, to rob a train. What a thrill it had been. Now he settled down to the practical aspect of outdistancing anyone who tried to give chase from the piddling little collection of shacks they called a town.

"Oh, yes, this is quite a day," he said. "To think that we pulled it off right in front of old Judge Roy Bean makes it even sweeter."

The man riding beside him was short and squat, with meat axe hands, half hooded eyes, and all the intelligence of a cedar fence post. But he was good with dynamite and had done his job perfectly. He had been hired for this one job, assured he would get a third of the loot, and that he would be on his way to California and well out of the way so no one could tie him to the robbery.

The money wasn't the important thing. He had wanted to do a robbery for the thrill—a train robbery, the way the Jessie James Gang did. To do it right on the doorstep of Judge Roy Bean was the gut-churning frosting on the robbery cake. Oh yes, no matter what was in the sacks of loot, it had been a great day.

Back at the joke of a town of Langtry, Texas, Judge Roy Bean himself examined the battered Express car. The sliding door had been blasted open with at least five sticks of dynamite, smashing the lock and jolting it along its tracks and slamming it off the rails to the ground.

The express agent had revived with no more damage than a pounding headache, and the realization that he would lose his job because his car had been looted. He sat on the floor, hands holding his head.

Judge Roy Bean had gained 40 unneeded pounds over the years and he huffed as he walked the length of the express car. He wore his usual white shirt, no tie, a black, single breasted suit coat, unbuttoned and held together at the top button hole with a heavy gold chain that stretched to the left top pocket where his gold-filled railroad watch lay.

His full beard and moustache had gone pure white several years ago, and now he kept it no more than an inch long, framing his face. His right eyelid dropped halfway down giving him a sleepy appearance. He always kept his soft brown hair cut short and businesslike.

The judge stopped in front of the cowering express clerk.

"Son, you get a good look at the pair?"

"No sir, the explosion put me in dreamland. I don't even remember the blast. I was walking along the outer door and next thing I know somebody threw water in my face where I lay on the floor of the car."

"Didn't see nary a hair of the pair?"

"Afraid not, Judge Bean. Sorry."

"Not your fault, son. Not your fault at all. Now you roust yourself up here, forget your troubles and tell us exactly what's missing so the twelve-oh-four can get highballing it down the line. What did they take?"

"The safe was open. I was putting in some new valuables. Looks like they cleaned that out. Let's see what else isn't here."

The clerk came to his knees, then stood with difficulty and stared at the bin where he kept the registered mail sacks. He had to sign off on each piece, and today he had two filled sacks. It would take him a half hour to sign off on them and get them into the next clerk's hands at the end of his run.

He frowned. He had the two sacks right there in the bin. With a wail of anger and fear he turned and searched the rest of the car. When he came back he shook his head.

"Judge, they got away with two sacks of registered mail. Folks send all sorts of valuables in them registered letters and packages. I'm in deep-shit trouble, Judge. You got to help me with the road. You got influence. You got to make them understand I didn't have no way of knowing anything would happen here and both doors was locked shut like always at a stop. You got to put in a good word for me, Judge."

Judge Roy Bean scowled, shot a deadly glance at the conductor who had his arms akimbo waiting for the judge to give him permission to move the train. Judge Bean waved the conductor out of the express car and then the judge stepped to the ground and nodded at the railroad man.

"Might as well move it, can't do no good here. I reckon the railroad detectives will be all over the place on the next run."

"Absolutely. Government might send in somebody, too, since it's a mail robbery. I'd say you gonna have your little town filled up with detectives afore long."

Judge Roy Bean nodded and the conductor hit the cinders and waved at the fireman who had laid out the dead engineer carefully, then grabbed the Johnson bar and levered the train into motion down the tracks.

A few minutes later, Judge Roy Bean sat on his porch again. Only the empty tracks and the little station showed where the train had been. He didn't like detectives smelling up his town. Damn, but they would come. He'd try not to let them bother him.

Eight days after the train robbery in Langtry, Texas, the Treasury Department of the United States Government realized that they had a problem.

For the first time, they had hired a talented engraver in San Francisco to engrave the printing plates for the new issue twenty-dollar bill. The plates were finished, front and back of the new twenty, and sent by registered mail from San Francisco through the southern route on the

Southern Pacific, to forestall any attempt to steal the plates.

Ordinarily, a courier would have the plates in a small leather case padlocked to his wrist and removable only with a duplicate key located in Washington, DC. This time the couriers in San Francisco were ill or on vacation and the plates had to be moved. Other valuable items had been shipped before by registered mail on express rail cars with no trouble. The decision was made in Washington to do so again.

Now, four days after the plates were due to arrive in Washington, DC, at the Bureau of Printing and Engraving, the plates had not arrived. Word was received of a train robbery in a small Texas waypoint where the plates had been stolen in one of two registered mail sacks.

Spur McCoy, a member of the Secret Service, had been cleaning up a small case in Portland, Oregon. He was immediately notified by telegram to proceed to San Antonio, Texas, where he would be given final instructions and then sent on to Langtry, Texas, to investigate the loss and attempt to regain the plates.

The telegram in Spur's hands spelled it out in unrelenting details of doom.

*If the plates fall into the wrong hands, the results could be devastating to the economy of the nation. Untold millions of dollars of bogus bills could be printed. Since the plates are perfect in every detail, the bills could be detected only by experts who would need to examine the paper used for the printing and the quality of the printing.*

*If the counterfeiters used a modern press*

*that could number each bill, it would be virtually impossible to identify the counterfeits. Millions upon millions of dollars of the bogus bills could be produced year after year with little hope of finding the perpetrators.*

Spur McCoy settled into the rail car seat and read a second telegram that had arrived from the Texas Rangers detailing what they knew about the case. They had been called in late and neither they, nor two men who had ridden out from Langtry immediately after the robbery, could track the culprits farther than the first creek where the tracks vanished in the water.

"Nothing to go on," Spur muttered under his breath. "Not a damn thing to go on and they expect me to bring back the plates?"

It took Spur three days of switching and changing roads and trains and cars until he at last arrived in San Antonio, Texas, where he met a member of the Texas Rangers who showed him all the evidence that he didn't have.

Spur growled as he paced the hotel room and stared at the Texas Ranger. "What you're telling me is you don't know anything about who robbed the train except there were two mounted men. You don't know where they went, who they were, or what happened to the registered mail?"

"Oh, we found some of that. Fact is we found most of it about halfway between Langtry and San Antonio. All of it had been torn open. Cash money had been stripped out of letters and envelopes and the two engravings were missing along with some stocks and bonds that can't be traced."

"Where did you find the trash?"

"Near a little town called River Junction, about thirty miles outside of town."

"Is the town on the Southern Pacific tracks?"

"Yes, but we think the pair came into San Antonio by horse to avoid any suspicion. They got to River Junction, took time out to sort through the registered mail, took the valuables, and discarded the rest in a gully a quarter of a mile from town. Some kids found it and told their parents."

"You've heard of fingerprints?" Spur asked.

"Yes, but we don't have the equipment to find them or to read or match them. Without a suspect, fingerprints don't do us any good anyway."

"What was in the safe?"

"About five-thousand in cash, bills mostly. Some stocks and bonds, three gold watches, old ones, collector's items highly valued. An interesting point here. Some of the stocks were almost worthless. They were discarded with the mail that was not valuable.

"So somebody knew his stocks and bonds. This wasn't a pair of shiftless cowpokes out to steal a few dollars." Spur went to the hotel room window and looked down on the street. San Antonio had blossomed since he'd been there last. It was a good sized town now.

"Any kind of action on finding the bogus bills?"

"Not our specialty. The Treasury Department said they have some people trained in those skills and would be sending one out here to watch for such bills."

"Treasury is sending someone here?"

"What my last wire said. The Secretary of the Treasury himself said that an expert named M.J.

Philburton should be here tomorrow."

Spur scowled. He hated working with anyone else. "This Philburton will be in tomorrow?"

"That's what the wire said. Philburton will contact you here at your hotel."

"Great, an expert on printing paper. Just what I need. In the meantime, where's the express car?"

"Down at the railyards here in San Antonio. It was coming this way so they left it here for repairs. We've been over it a thousand times. The pair left nothing on board that will help. You're free to take a look."

"I will. Did anyone speak with either of the robbers?"

"No, they shot and killed the engineer with rifles from long range, then blew out the door with dynamite, stole the goods, fired shotguns at any train workers trying to get forward, mounted up and rode away firing behind them. Three trainmen fired rifles at them as they galloped away but all rounds missed. The trainmen had no horses to launch a pursuit. Nobody in town really wanted to ride out after them, but two men at last took a look. They came up empty. That's it."

"So no up-close witnesses. The express clerk was unconscious, and they got away clean. Great."

"This expert from Washington, DC, is supposed to arrive tomorrow. I hope that he can help."

"Has anyone seen any fake bills showing up yet?" Spur asked.

"No reports. Not in our jurisdiction, but we haven't heard anything about any phoney money."

"Eleven days since the robbery," Spur mused out loud. "Plenty of time to get a press cranked up and the ink dry on a sheet of twenty-dollar bills. Any good printers in town?"

The Texas Ranger shook his head. "Not what I could guarantee, sorry. I've seen two or three around. Heard some of them do fine work, but printing money is another thing. Who would risk going to prison for twenty years?"

"Oh, there'll be somebody. Those plates could be worth ten million dollars if the person who has them does it right. He prints the cash in one town, then deposits it or spends it in a dozen different towns within two or three weeks. Then he wires the bank and has the funds transferred to another bank and lays low for a couple of months. Soon he does it all again in another section of the country. I've seen too much of it."

The ranger grinned. "Good luck. I can't help you any more."

A half hour later, Spur McCoy checked in at the lead man's shack at the railyards, then went to inspect the battered express car sitting on a back siding. Two men were about to start the repair job. They checked the ripped apart door and shook their heads.

"Where was the charge placed?" Spur asked.

"You a detective or something?"

"Yep. Did the dynamite go right on the outside door latch?"

"That's my guess from the ripped up metal," the taller of the two men said. "Powerful charge the way it curled and twisted this heavy steel."

"Five sticks?" Spur asked.

"Not five sticks of the usual twenty percent ordinary dynamite," the trainman said. "I used to be a powder man in a hard rock mine. For solid rock, we used what we called red-line charges. We was a little operation so we didn't have it made special. It was regular sixty-percent dynamite, with a lot more nitro in it."

"Sixty percent?"

"Right. It would do this kind of damage to steel. Let's take a look. Usually there's some of the outside wrapping of the dynamite blasted against part of the wreckage."

They examined the damaged door that had been returned to them, as well as the near side of the place the door latched. They found nothing unusual.

Spur checked the shattered door again and looked deeper into the hollow core of the heavy door. He thought he saw something. He pulled out a match, lit it and pushed the lit end into the hollow space of the door. A moment later he pulled out a jagged piece of heavy paper just over an inch square.

The paper had a thin red line through it and some numbers printed in black ink. He showed it to the trainman who grinned.

"Damn, you did fine. I saw you pull that out of the door there. Good thinking. That's what I'd call a great clue. Unless they've changed their methods, that's sixty-percent dynamite from the Atlas Powder Company in Houston. They make it, wholesale it to mining outfits, some to general stores and hardware stores.

"What about here in San Antonio?"

"About the only place you could find it would be at the Texas State Mining Supplies on Third Avenue."

"The numbers?" Spur asked.

"Lot numbers. If you have all the numbers the

company can tell you where that lot was sold, to what retail store."

Spur thanked the men and headed toward Third Avenue. He'd seen the store. It held almost everything a hard rock miner could use, including ore cars, track, hoists, cable, chain, and dynamite.

He entered the store. It even smelled like a mine. He found a clerk near the back and asked him about 60-percent dynamite.

The clerk looked up with a slight frown. "Sure, we can get it. Special order from Houston, the factory. Don't sell much of it, too damn dangerous. We had two men killed on one batch of 60-percent we sold a year ago. Owner doesn't like to sell it unless he knows the operation. What mine you with?"

"I'm not with any mine. I'm an investigator looking into the use of some sixty-percent." He showed the man the square of paper. The man sniffed it and nodded. "We call it red line."

"Have you sold any in the last month or so?"

"I'll check the order book, right back here." They moved into a small office and the man looked in a book with a red cover. He nodded. "Two orders for red line in the last month. We got ten cases for the Deep Ridge Mine about fifty miles out of town. They picked it up just a month ago. Old line outfit we work with all the time.

"The other order was for one case, fifty sticks. Ordered and picked up by Tom Jones."

"Any address on this Jones?"

"Nope. He paid cash, we ordered it and he picked it up ten days later and took it away."

"You remember anything about him?"

"Can't say I do. I didn't write the order or

deliver it. We get over a hundred customers a day through here. Sometimes it's a madhouse."

"When was it delivered?"

"June fourth, about three weeks ago now."

"Thanks. Oh, I need that torn chunk of paper from the red line." Spur took a five-dollar bill from his wallet and folded it twice and held it out to the clerk. "Ask around and see if you can find who did order that red line. There's twenty more if the man who ordered it can remember anything about the customer. I'll be back tomorrow. The fiver is for you."

The clerk grabbed the bill which represented a week's wages and pushed it in his pocket before anyone else could notice it.

"Yes sir, I'll surely ask around. Should be able to find him. Oh, you have a name?"

"McCoy, Spur McCoy. I'll be back tomorrow hunting some good news."

Spur marched out the door to the street and turned left. So far it had not been a good day. Almost four in the afternoon. Nothing more could go wrong today. He had one slender, slim lead. Tomorrow he'd start talking to printers, see if any of them were nervous. As for tonight, he wanted to rest up after a hectic three day train ride, eat a delicious supper, then take a long hot bath and settle in for ten hours of sleep. Then he'd be ready to tackle tomorrow.

San Antonio wasn't so big yet that he couldn't walk to his hotel. After a ten minute stroll he stepped into the hotel and asked for his key at the desk. The key was gone from his box. The clerk looked at him.

"Room 212, Mr. McCoy?"

"That's right. I left the key here. Must have been misplaced."

The clerk rummaged in a drawer and found another key tagged with the 212 number and gave it to Spur.

Upstairs he pushed the key in the lock and twisted it. As always, he stood on the wall side of the door in case anyone wanted to greet him with a shotgun blast. Nothing happened as he unlocked the barrier. He pushed the door open so it hit the far wall. Nobody hiding there.

He peered around the wall, saw no one and stepped into the room.

As he did, a pretty, young woman moved away from the inside wall where she had been standing.

She grinned. "About time you got here, McCoy. I arrived a day early. I'm Treasury Agent M.J. Philburton."

# Chapter Two

Spur McCoy stood just inside the door to his room so shocked he couldn't take another step. He scowled and shook his head.

"Miss, you say you're with the Treasury Department, that you're a field agent?"

"Exactly, McCoy. I'm not Secret Service like you are, but I've had field training and I'm one of the two top experts on U.S. Government currency printing dealing with ink and paper. Have any of the suspected bogus bills shown up yet?"

Spur lifted his brows and took a better look at the young woman. He figured her at about 30 years old and she had her wheat blonde hair cut short with bangs across her forehead. She was slender, with a well filled white blouse and a pretty face that now grinned as he checked her soft blue eyes.

"Damn, I hope I pass inspection. I'd hate to

be sent back to Washington because I was too fat, too stupid or too ugly. What's my evaluation score?"

Spur unfroze and grinned. "I was just surprised at you being a woman. M.J. Philburton figured to be a male, but obviously you're not. Your evaluation score?" Spur chuckled and closed the door. She didn't even seem to notice. "I'd have to give you about a ninety-nine on my scorecard but that's only for appearance, demeanor and voice quality. I don't know if you can shoot the .38 revolver you have in your reticule, or how good you really are on picking out counterfeit paper and inks."

"That part is easy. The first impression was what I was a little worried about. Have you had supper yet? If not, I'm buying. I'm on an expense account, too. Do you know the best place in town to eat?"

They dined at the hotel because it was convenient. He quickly learned that she had a room two doors down from his and that she had lifted the key to his room after finding out which space he was in. Spur also found out she was bright, educated, from an old Washington family of an ex Senator from New York, that she had been born and raised in Washington and grew up hearing nothing but politics and political maneuvering.

She had taken off her traveling jacket and Spur noticed how her breasts pushed delightfully against the tight white blouse. The top button on the blouse had come undone and she didn't bother to refasten it.

He had a steak and she settled for a pair of pork chops. They had covered the things most people talk about when they first meet including family, schools, first jobs and how they got into the present work. She picked up her fork and pointed it at him.

"So, I might as well get this out right at the start. "I'm thirty-one years old. I've never been married, and I am not thinking about it right now. I have a great job and it's exciting and stimulating. I do enjoy the company of men."

Spur nearly choked on a bite of steak. He got it chewed and swallowed and saw her watching him with amusement.

"I hope I didn't embarrass you."

Spur smiled and nodded. "So it's up to me to tell you that I enjoy the charms of a lovely woman. Now you're informed and warned. What I really want to know is how you can spot a twenty dollar bill that's a fake?"

He took out his wallet and laid out three twenty dollar greenbacks and motioned to them. "Which one is the counterfeit?"

She glanced at him and smiled. "Thanks for the warning. Of course I don't know your taste in women, but I'm sufficiently alerted. Now to work."

She picked up the first bank note and studied the front, then the back. She laid it down and examined the other two bills the same way. Then she wadded them up and straightened them out.

"Did I do that critically enough for you? The one in the center is the counterfeit. That's an obvious fake, bad printing, wrong ink color and the engraving is wrong around the forehead and face. Then there's the number. It's one digit short. In training we called this the famous and well known short number bill. You might be surprised that they still use it as an example in the training classes."

Spur put the bills back in his wallet, folding the fake one and slipping it into a separate compartment.

"I used to carry one of those, then one day I spent it accidentally and they won't give me another one."

They both laughed.

"I understand you've only been in town part of today. Do we have anything to go on yet?"

"Not much." He hesitated. "Did your boss tell you that I don't like to work with anyone on a case. I work alone. Whatever you dig up will be appreciated, but don't think we're going to be pulling in double harness here."

"Oh, I have been warned about your lone-wolf behavior. I'm used to being discriminated against just because I'm a woman. All I have to do is win your confidence, show you I can do the job and then we'll have no problems."

"If and when you do convince me."

"What do we have so far?" She stared at him, her open, pretty face showing a touch of strain. Her eyes seemed to turn into a deeper steely blue, little frown lines showed around her eyes and her mouth tightened. The expression made her round face with high cheekbones even more attractive.

"Not much. I'm tracking down the high-powered dynamite that was used on the express car door. I want to grab the robbers and their printer before they know how valuable those plates are."

"Any hope to get to them before they start printing?"

"Not much. It's been eleven days now since the robbery. Say five days into San Antonio by horseback and then they still have to find a printer they can trust. They must realize what the plates are or they wouldn't have taken them. So all we do now is hope."

"Or wait for the first bills to circulate."

"Would you print them here and try to pass some of them here?" Spur asked.

"A few, to see how easy it was going to be. I'd even fake a bad knee and ask a kindly little old lady to take one of the fake twenties into a bank and ask for change. If they figured out it was a fake, I'd be a mile away before they got the little old lady out the front door to point me out."

Spur nodded. "You'd have made a good criminal. It's not too late to change professions. All we have to do is find those plates and take off for Mexico and print up all the cash we want and live like royalty."

"I'm afraid I can't do that. My Spanish isn't that good. Anyway, I'm enjoying my work too much to leave."

"At least we have that settled. Now, how can you spot a bad bill by the paper? Isn't the kind of paper the government uses available to other printers?"

"Not the exact paper. The formula and pattern and diagrams in the paper itself are all unique. Some similar paper is made, but it's expensive and we have a list of everyone who buys it. Usually it's used for expensive certificates, bonds, stocks, that sort of thing."

"So you find the fake paper by the feel?"

"Sometimes. Often the quality of the green ink is a giveaway, sometimes the paper. We have those two things to watch for. The third key is the serial number. If they print more than one bill with the same serial number, we eventually find it and then we can watch for that serial number."

"Too much work. I'd rather grab them before they can print."

"Ideal, but in this case you don't have a single clue to go on."

"I have one. They used sixty-percent dynamite, not the usual twenty percent, and it's a special order item. Sold here in town. I have people trying to remember the customer."

"Phoney name?"

"Tom Jones, as fake as you can get. But I'll find him. He's still got about forty sticks of that sixty-percent powder out there somewhere."

"I can't do much until we get one of the bills to start working on. My first job in the morning will be to go visit all of the banks in town and check their twenties, then tell them what to watch for. Might not work. Usually doesn't. But sometimes we get lucky and find a bill the first day they start passing them."

Spur took a last sip of coffee. The meal was over. He didn't know why they didn't leave.

"It bothers you, doesn't it, having to work with a woman."

"We're not working together, we're simply assigned to the same case. You have your area of work and I have mine."

She frowned slightly and her next words came with deliberation. "But don't you think sooner or later we'll be working closely together on some aspect of the case?"

Spur gave a small sigh and looked at her, then away and back to her again. "Miss Philburton, I don't see how that would happen. If I find the robber, he'll lead me to the printer and to the plates. If you find some of the money, it probably won't lead us anywhere, we'll simply know that it's here. The robbers are the key to the case, not the paper on the street."

Color flared in her face and she stiffened. "We'll see about that, Mr. McCoy. Now, if you're through, I think it's time we leave."

"Don't forget to pay at the counter."

She looked at him with surprise, then a bit of anger. "You're actually going to let me pay for your dinner?"

"Absolutely. I wouldn't deny you the pleasure. After all, you did invite me to the meal. I thank you for the fine steak. Oh, you can have them charge it to your room."

The color rose higher in her cheeks and M.J. Philburton arose quickly and walked to the desk near the entrance where she spoke with the woman working there. Spur grinned as he came up behind her, approved of the saucy little rump showing through her tight skirt and passed on to the lobby.

She caught up with him a moment later.

"I hope you're satisfied. You embarrassed me in front of those people. That must have been what you intended. I don't care. I've been embarrassed by better men than you."

"But have you bought them a steak dinner?" Spur chuckled and caught her elbow. "Allow me to escort you to your room. Never know who you might meet out here in the wild west."

She pulled away a moment, then gave in and they walked up the stairs.

A small smile dented her frown. She looked up. "Oh, since we're going to be working together so closely, you can call me Marci."

"Marci, good. Call me Spur."

"You enjoyed doing that, didn't you? Embarrassing me that way."

"Not true, it was what you decided to do. I just let you do what you said you would do when you invited me to supper."

"I've said that a dozen times in Washington and not once did I have to pay for the meal."

"This is the wild west, lady. We play our cards different out here."

"All right, I give up. Oh, I have a letter for you in my luggage. Why don't I give it to you right now. I think it's from your chief at the Secret Service."

She found her key in her reticule, unlocked the door and stepped in. She looked back to where he stood in the hall. "You can come in, I'm not going to be a black widow spider."

Spur nodded and stepped inside but left the door open. Her leather traveling case on the bed had been left open and he saw a variety of silk underthings. She stepped in front of the bag and took something from the other side, then closed the bag. She turned and gave him a long envelope.

"I guess this qualifies me to be in the Postal Department as well."

He took the letter, looked at the return and saw the familiar name of the Capital Investigations and the D.C. address they used sometimes to conceal the real identity of the service.

Marci watched him a moment then sighed and shook her head.

"Spur, I was hoping we could get along. I see that we have a small problem. It isn't just that you want to work alone and you don't want to work with a woman.

"We've been at each other like jealous lovers for the past hour. I can't do my best work this way, and I'd guess that you can't either. Let's get it out in the open. I'll say what I'm feeling if you will."

She looked at him and he nodded. "Fine. What are you feeling?"

Marci looked away a moment, then stepped closer to him and looked him in the eye. "At my first sight of you I was impressed by your stature and your amazing good looks. You have a subtle charm that stirs me. Right now I'm wondering what it would be like to kiss you. I think this is something we should get out of the way now so it won't pop up later and interfere with our assignment here. There, I've said it."

Spur bent forward and without touching her any other place, gently kissed her lips. Her eyes closed and she sighed and leaned forward. He let up on the kiss and her eyes stayed shut for a moment, then opened.

"You want me to be honest?" he asked. She nodded. "I liked the kiss. When I first saw you in my room I wondered who the pretty girl was. I was intrigued by your fine figure and your great breasts. And I wondered what it would be like to hold you tight and kiss you."

His arms came around her and he pressed her body hard against his until her breasts flattened against his chest. Their lips met, hers came open and his tongue darted inside as she sighed again. Her knees buckled but he pulled her tightly against him. He held the kiss a long time and they both ran out of breath. He let up and she opened her eyes and stared at him. Then her knees buckled again.

"I think that we better sit down on the bed or

I'm going to crumple up on the floor."

He took two steps with her and they sat on the bed close together. She pushed her leg hard against his.

"Oh, Spur McCoy, now that was a kiss. Don't you think we should clear up this little misunderstanding we have right now, right here, so it doesn't hurt the case?"

"I think that would be a fine idea, Marci. How do we clear it up?"

She reached up and kissed his lips a dozen times with little nibble kisses, then eased back and caught one of his hands and put it over her breast.

"Let's clear it up with a little caressing and some more delicious kisses."

Spur's lips found hers and he eased her back on the bed until she was flat on her back. He stretched out half on top of her. Through it all he still held the kiss and she sighed again and pushed her hips over until they pressed against his side. His hand kept working at her breast and she made small noises in her throat and nodded.

"Yes, Spur McCoy. I think this is the way to get rid of our hostility and to become better friends."

His hand opened two buttons on her white blouse and worked under the silky chemise he found there until he could close his fingers around one of her big, bare breasts.

Marci trembled. She looked at him, her face serious. "Oh, yes, Spur, that feels so fine. It's marvelous when you pet me that way. My titties just want you to caress them forever."

She kissed him again and her tongue drove into his mouth. He let her explore, then pushed her out and penetrated her mouth with his tongue. She sighed again.

He found her hand and put it down to the lump behind his fly. She smiled and began to open the buttons there.

A moment later she pulled his hand away from her breast and sat up, her blue eyes flashing.

"Spur McCoy. I don't want you to think that I flip up my skirts for just anyone. I'm a grown woman and I have some sexual needs, but I don't bed every man who comes along. I'm no virgin, but I'm not a wanton either. It's been over six months since the last time I made love. How long has it been for you?"

"Not important. I understand what you're saying. I do think you're right about this being a fine way to lessen any animosity between us." He bent and kissed her. Then he pushed lower and kissed her breast through the fabric. She moaned softly and lay down on the bed, her hands undoing the rest of the buttons on her blouse and pushing back the cloth to both sides.

He lifted her silk chemise and smiled at her full breasts. They had small areolas of light pink but sturdy standing tall nipples of bright red where they had filled with hot, fresh blood.

"Kiss my titties now," she said.

He started at the outside where they began to rise and circled them with kisses, working around and around until he came to the very top where he licked her nipple and then nibbled at it gently until she wailed. Then he moved to her other breast and repeated the ritual.

Her breathing quickened and she grabbed his hand and pulled it between her parted legs. She had lifted her skirts around her waist and he felt her upper legs, then the silky fabric of her bloomers. She pressed his hand hard against her crotch and when he touched the wetness of her as his fingers touched her moist outer lips through the silk, she erupted into a jolting climax. Her voice keened high and long and then her body shook with a series of spasms that jolted her again and again until she whimpered at the force of them. She quieted a moment and she pressed his fingers against her most private part again. She thundered into another long series of climaxes that continued for two or three minutes and left her panting and quaking. She put her arms around him, rolled over on top of him and hugged him as her breathing slowly returned to normal.

Marci sat up and he went with her. She stared at him with wide eyes and a tear formed in one eye and slowly worked down her cheek. She reached in and kissed his cheek, then his soft lips and then bent and kissed the rodlike bulge behind his fly.

"Never before have I done that. No man has ever excited me the way you do and it frightens me. No one has ever aroused me to such heights without even penetrating me. It's awesome, it's something important I have to consider carefully and evaluate.

"I'm sorry I didn't give you a chance. But I'm absolutely wasted and used up and I can't stand being in heat a moment longer. Please, would you leave? I know it's asking a lot after getting you all worked up, but you'll recover. You're much stronger than I am. Please, can I ask you to leave?"

He stood and she came up beside him. "Just one last kiss," she said. "Soft and gentle and serious."

Spur bent and brushed her lips with his so lightly that at first she may not have been sure he touched her, but the electricity danced between their lips and she let out a little cry and stared at him in wonder.

Spur watched her a moment, then turned and walked out the door to his own room down the hall. He had felt his own desire slackening as she had talked to him. Now he was soft and relaxed as he stripped down to his underwear and lay on top of the sheet on the short bed. When would they make beds that would be comfortable for a man over six feet tall?

Marci had been right. There had been a sexual tension between them from the moment they met. Now most of it would be gone. Now they could work together and he knew that they would. She was smart and sharp, and would find any counterfeits if they were circulating in town.

Spur blew out the coal-oil lamp, closed his eyes and moved into his sleep position, flat on his back with his right hand under his pillow within inches of his loaded and cocked .45 Colt revolver. It had been a good half day on site of the case.

Tomorrow he had to find out at least a description of the man who bought the 60-percent dynamite from the mining store. Tomorrow. He had to find those plates and the men who now owned them.

If they were not recovered they could eventually result in hundreds of millions of dollars in un-backed paper money in circulation and that could bring down the government. Tomorrow. He had to find the man who bought that sixty-percent red line dynamite!

He sat up in the bed and scowled into the

blackness of the hotel room. The damn letter that she had brought from the General. What did the letter say? He could read it now or in the morning. It was still in his shirt pocket. He remembered feeling it when he had stripped out of his shirt. Spur thought about it a minute, decided it couldn't be anything vital or the general would have told her to have him read it and make an immediate reply.

# Chapter Three

Spur's bare feet hit the floor at six-thirty and he cranked his eyelids up so he could find his britches. Brown town pants, a fresh tan shirt, his naked leather vest and cowhand boots completed his wardrobe.

He shaved in cold water from the crockery pitcher and bowl and only cut himself once with the folding straight razor. He had just finished drying off his face when he remembered the letter from the general.

Spur sat on the bed and unfolded the two pager written in the general's all but unreadable hand.

*McCoy: The President is worried about the missing plates. He says it could lead to a collapse of the currency and bankruptcy for millions.*

*Consequently, I have asked Treasury to*

*send their top expert on counterfeiting to work with you. No horse hockey about how you work alone. This is such a horrendous problem that we need all the help that's available.*

*Tie down the culprits and recover the plates or see that they are destroyed as quickly as possible. Ideal timing would be to prevent any of the counterfeited bills from reaching circulation.*

*Advise soonest of any problems. Government vouchers in the amount of 500 dollars enclosed. Keep strict accounting of all monies spent. Spare no effort to terminate this threat to the currency.*

Spur fastened on his gunbelt, slid the .45 Colt in place and checked to be sure the twenty cartridges were in the belt loops. He settled the holster low on his thigh, tied down the thong on the bottom around his leg and tested it. Yes. He could draw quickly and the leather home of his Colt did not rise more than a quarter of an inch.

He picked up his hat, a black flat brim with a low crown and silver Mexican pesos strung around it as a headband, and went out the door. Spur McCoy stood two inches over six feet with a sturdy build of nearly 200 pounds of lean fighting muscle. His dark hair fringed his ears and he wore it a little longer than the average businessman, but his sideburns never grew below his ear lobes.

Otherwise he was clean shaven with a strong nose, once broken, and serious green eyes. He had good hands, was a top-notch horseman and could earn his living as a working cowhand if he had to. He was an excellent shot with a six-gun, rifle and shotgun and knew more than a dozen ways to kill a man with his bare hands.

He had graduated from Harvard, spent a year in one of his father's import-export stores in New York City and then went into the army for a hitch as an Infantry officer.

He joined the Secret Service as one of its first members, and now was an old hand with all the nation west of the Mississippi as his territory of responsibility.

He paused two doors down the hall at room 216 and then knocked on the wood. Nothing happened. He knocked again.

A sleepy voice came through the panel.

"Who is it?"

"Spur, you had breakfast?"

"No, but you can't come in. I'm not decent."

"Good, let me in. You were lots better than decent last night."

"No, now go away. I'll see you in the dining room."

She came down ten minutes later as bright as a spring sunflower, all smiles and flashing white teeth and a red silk blouse that looked as if it would burst open at any moment. It was buttoned to her neck and had long sleeves.

He nodded. "Morning. Glad I waited to see you."

"Thank you, kind gentleman. You haven't eaten?"

"Waiting for a pretty lady to join me. She finally came. You want the ranch house breakfast?"

"Is there a lot of it?"

"There is, and I'm buying."

"Good."

He held up two fingers and the waiter, who had been watching, hurried into the kitchen.

They sipped coffee waiting for the meal. "How well do you know the President?" Spur asked.

"I've only met him once in a receiving line. He wouldn't know me from his great Aunt Tootsie's second cousin from Texas. You know him?"

"We've met a time or two. I rode shotgun for him a few times. He's worried about these engravings."

"He should be. It could be a disaster. Somebody could print off a hundred million dollar's worth, keep it for five years, then pass it through banks and we'd have no way to find it or to stop them."

"You still don't want to take the plates and ride off with me to Mexico?"

"Afraid not."

"Then I guess I'm saddled with you. My chief asked your boss to assign the best man he had."

"That should be best 'person.' I thought we established that last night." She grinned and a dimple sank into her right cheek.

"We halfway established it."

She closed her eyes a moment in what he decided was a ladylike display of mock embarrassment, then ignored his remark. "What are you going to do today?"

"The dynamite. It's got to be a lead. It's all I have as a clue and now I must rely on some merchant's clerks to remember the man."

"They might surprise you."

The food came. It was on twelve-inch plates piled high with three fried eggs, a heap of country fried potatoes, six slices of bacon, three hot cakes with butter melting on top, two sausage patties, a pot of coffee, three slices of toast and a platter with an assortment of jams.

"Hungry?" Spur asked.

They both emptied their plates.

At the pay counter, she watched him. "Contact point. Shall we make it the lobby, or in here for coffee?"

"Coffee at noon and then we'll go out for dinner, lunch to you easterners."

She nodded. "I'll be doing the banks. I know how to get in the side doors before they open. I flash my Treasury Department identification card." She waved and walked away and Spur watched her tight little bottom swaying just enough as she moved to the door. It was a beautiful sight.

He took his change from the cashier and headed for the mining store. They probably opened at seven.

He had talked to four clerks before he had any kind of luck.

"Yeah, I took the order. Then I delivered the goods. He had a small little hack I've seen a dozen times before. People rent it two blocks down at the San Antonio Livery when they need a rig to haul something."

"You get a good look at him?"

"Sure, I took his money, then carried the box out to his hack. He had long hair, like one them mountain men, and the strange part was it wasn't nowhere near the color of his beard. Wore a full beard, dull black and about an inch long all over. Sideburns, moustache, the whole thing."

"Could his hair have been a wig?"

"Hey, never thought of that. Sure, now that I ponder it a bit. The hair could have been pinned on somehow but the beard was real. He was scratching it about the way I used to before I went naked faced. Another thing, this guy was tall and thin and he had a tanned face and kind of funny looking eyes."

"You get any kind of an address, any idea what he wanted the strong powder for?"

"Said he had a small place out north of town in the foothills and he had to break up some rocks so he could build a new barn. I should be able to find the order in our book. We write all them specials down so we don't lose them. Want me to look?"

Five minutes later the clerk put his finger on a line. "Here it is, May fourth, one case of 60-percent red line. Tom Jones was the name he used. No address. Note says he'd check back in a week. He picked up the powder on May tenth. I initialled the delivery so we can keep our records straight."

"You said he had a place north of town. He look like a farmer to you?"

"Him, not a chance. His hands were clean and no callouses, no rope burns either like a cowboy would have. He looked like a dandy to me. Had on suit pants, black ones, better than any of my Sunday meeting clothes. Wore a plaid shirt but it didn't seem right on him."

"How did he talk? Rough and crude?"

"Oh, not a chance. He talked damn near like a sissy. I mean, he used perfect grammar like I never learned. His voice was calm and controlled. I dropped the damn case about a foot and he went white and near shit his pants. I figured he didn't know much about powder, especially the sixty-percent red line."

"Which direction did he head when he left?"

"Strange thing, he didn't. Just sat there holding the reins until I got in the store. I figured the hell with him, I didn't need to know which way he went."

Spur gave the man the 20 dollar bill, accepted a handshake of thanks and stepped out the back door to the alley. Less than a month ago, on May tenth, the train robber was in this alley. Which way did he go? Did he go back to the same place where he lived after the robbery?

The livery. He'd check to see if they kept any records. The odds weren't good on that. He walked down three blocks on First Avenue and found the livery. As usual, it had pastures and corrals in back that angled out into the open country.

A small office just inside the big barn doors held one man bent over a desk. Spur tapped on the door and went in. The man looked up. He had a full white moustache and white hair.

"Aye, yep. What in hell can I do for you?"

Spur grinned, liking the old cus at once. "Like to buy you a beer but the nearest saloon is too far off."

"Booze and me ain't a bit friendly no more. I leave the guzzling up to you young bucks. What else you want?"

"I'm interested in a hack you rented on May tenth to a tall thin man with good manners, prissy ways and extremely correct speech. Remember any jay-bird like that?"

"Hey, jasper, I ain't no bank and no damn accountant either. I don't keep them kind of records. You want to know how much I took in that day I can tell you, but not a hell of a lot more."

"What I guessed." Spur dropped into a chair near the desk. "This is damn important. The man's a robber on a grand scale. Figured you could use part of the reward."

The word perked up the old man and he sat tall in his chair and rubbed his forehead. "That shitty little hack I don't rent out much. Too small for most folks who got something to haul. Women want a buggy to do a little tote job, men like a wagon. Damn little hack ain't been out of the yard more than two or three times." He paused and scowled.

"Run this jasper past me again, son. Might be the gray matter can get together on something."

"Heard him called tall and Texas thin, might have had a heavy black beard on the short side. Soft hands, not a farmer or rancher. Used precise English and I'd guess was soft spoken. Had a tanned face, probably from the East."

The old man started to laugh, then he wheezed and went into a coughing fit. He turned and spat into a copper spittoon near his desk. "Damn lungs got nothing inside them but cotton these days." He took several long and deep breaths and his breathing returned to normal.

"Yeah, that bit about soft spoken rings my belfry. The sod talked so quiet I had to make him repeat everything he said. He got a little put out and turned red in the face and stalked away, Then came back and paid for the rig and I had it hitched up and he drove down the street. Damn queer appearing gent. Tall, thin, black beard and short black hair. Had marks on each side of a long thin nose that looked like he wore spectacles."

"Any idea where he lives?"

The old livery man chuckled. "Might have.

Didn't trust that one so I made him give me a ten-dollar deposit and an address. He said it was 200 Fourth Avenue. I recollect that 'cause there ain't no houses or hotels on the second block on Fourth. Lived here all my life since San Antone was a cross roads. He thought again and said right it wasn't two hundred, it was 320 Fourth. Which could be. Don't keep records much, but something I wants to remember, by crackies, I can remember."

Spur thanked the old man who simply grinned and waved and then went back to his account books.

It took Spur ten minutes to find 320 Fourth Avenue. Fourth was two over from the main thoroughfare, and had businesses the first two blocks, then two rooming houses and two small houses spotted along the next block, the 300 one.

He looked over the two room and board houses. One two stories, the other three. Large places of wooden construction with porches around two sides. A rooming house would be too public for the men he looked for. They'd need more privacy than that to set up their scheme, store the bills, make plans for passing them.

He walked up a gravel path to the small house between the larger ones, and knocked on the front door. It took several moments for a small, older woman with a cane to answer the door.

"What is it, sonny?" she cracked.

"Is this the house that's for rent? The man downtown didn't give me good directions."

"For rent? Land o'goshen, not a chance. It's my house. Own it free and clear. Heard the small house two doors down had some new folks in it.

The Jackson's rent it out from time to time."

"New folks. A family?"

"Not that you could notice. I figure it for one man. Onlyest one I've seen come or go. Not that I sit here all day watching, you know. A body has things to get done, dishes, cooking, sewing a bit."

"Yes ma'am, I understand. Could you describe this man for me? Is he short and fat?"

"Oh, my no. He's tall. Not as tall as you, and thin. Seemed to be a good dresser. Wore one of them felt town hats."

"Well, guess it doesn't matter much if it's already rented. You sure he's still there. Maybe he moved."

"Nope. Saw him plain and clear not an hour ago. Had a little leather bag he was carrying like folks tote papers around in."

"Well, I guess I'll have to look somewhere else. It's been good chatting with you."

He checked the numbers on the houses as he continued past the second board and room establishment and then the rental beyond. None of them was numbered 320. The request for an address must have caught the robber by surprise and he blurted out the street without thinking, then tried to cover it up with a fake number. Caught on the 200, he had to invent a 300 number. Good, his first mistake.

Why a hack in the first place? Fifty sticks of dynamite wasn't that big a load. He could have carried it. More evidence that he was an Easterner or a city man. Then too, maybe he didn't want anyone to see him walking around with all that red line dynamite. Enough little mistakes by the robber would end with a big one, and Spur would have him.

Spur went well beyond the house, cut through to the next block and walked to where he could see the back door of the suspect house. There were no structures on this side of the block. Spur turned and walked toward the house's back door as if he belonged there.

A quick look inside the house might turn up some hard evidence against the man. Then he'd watch the place until the man returned. Simply picking up the robber wouldn't solve the problem. He would still have to find the printer.

Spur knew he was getting ahead of himself. He stepped into the back door and listened. No reaction, no noise. Quietly, he searched the five rooms. It had evidently been rented furnished. The furniture was all old and nondescript, but serviceable. On the kitchen table, he found a leather carrying case for papers, but nothing in it that would indicate the owner was the train robber. He found no engraving plates, no samples of printed bills, nothing to incriminate the man in the robbery of the twenty-dollar bill engravings.

Spur left the same way he came in. The person who lived there would not know he had been visited. He probably wouldn't return until tonight sometime. He could be at his printer right now. That was the next step, to check out the printers in town. Spur stopped by at the first one he came to on First Avenue.

San Antonio Printing, the sign read. Inside he found a counter and the smell of paper and ink and an attractive brunette woman asking if she could help him. He nodded.

"Yes, you can. I'm hunting the best printer in town. I have some delicate and intricate printing work I need done in two colors. Do you do colored ink jobs?"

"Yes, we do. We have a fine reputation here in town. Why don't you tell me exactly what you want done, how many copies and what colors of ink, and I'll work up an estimated cost for you. I think you'll find we can meet almost anyone's price for quality work."

Spur outlined what he wanted. He quickly made up the idea for a 20 by 30 inch broadside ad for an upcoming acting troupe. He wanted it in three colors and on stiff cardboard that could be stood up in windows and tacked to trees and buildings to advertise the touring group.

The woman excused herself and went to a desk where she checked in some small books and leaflets to establish the cost and their price. As she did, Spur looked around. It was evidently a two person shop, the woman in front and one man in back working two small hand bed presses. No complicated equipment, not a big stock of paper. Not a good candidate for his counterfeit printer.

The woman came back smiling. "We can't do a piece that large on our presses, but we can do an 8 ½ by 22. That would give you a good proportion for your broadside. I've worked out our cost figures."

Spur shook his head. "Sorry, I really need the larger size. Can you suggest another printer that might be able to do it?"

"I'm sorry, we're fairly new in town and I don't know the other printers that well."

He thanked her and left the store and moved down the street. How many printers were in town? The post office could help him. He found the sign for the mail place on a hardware store and went inside. The postmistress went behind her small cage and he showed her his Secret Service credentials.

"This is confidential and extremely sensitive. I need to know the names and addresses of the printers in town. Can you help me?"

The woman was a little flustered by the government identification and the fact that something might be wrong, but she wrote down for him the four names of printers in San Antonio including that of the local newspaper. He ruled that one out at once, they had too much to lose. He thanked her and marched out to the first name on the list. He'd have time before meeting Marci for lunch. Lunch, he'd said it. The term was more and more coming into use. But most Texans and midwesterners still had breakfast, dinner and supper. Lunch was something for the fancy San Francisco matrons and the New York Society ladies.

Ambrose Printing looked like a one-man operation, and it was. A bell over the door tinkled as he went in. Again the smell of paper and ink assaulted him, but he quickly became used to it.

The place looked like a Texas tornado had hit the paper supply. It was all over the counter on boxes, in the corner, along one wall on a makeshift table on sawhorses. Paper in a dozen different shades and colors. At first he saw no one but heard the metallic ring of a press in operation. He peered around to see where the sound came from.

He found an old hand press cranking away behind a stub wall. A man in a green eyeshade looked up and stopped the press.

"Uh, didn't see you come in. Whatda ya want?"

"I had thought of getting some printing done, but it's a delicate job, three colors, three press runs. You ever do work like that?"

"Not usual. Nobody hereabouts can afford it. I'm the cheapest printer in town. Damn proud of it, but I still do good work. I put in long hours, nobody but me to pay and I save left over paper so I can cut my paper costs on the next job. I ain't one of them printers who throws out good paper just because I cut it off on my hand slicer and it's not a full nine by twelve."

"From the stacks of paper you have in stock, I can understand that. I think I'll check out the other printers."

Spur turned to leave but the small man in the green eyeshade wasn't done.

"Whatever they say they can print it for, I can do it for twenty-percent less, no lie. Come back and let me bid on it after you get to the other jackasses and see their charges."

Spur waved and went out the door.

Lunch time. No, damn it—dinner time. Almost noon. He never made it to the Drake Hotel coffee shop. Marci Philburton waved him down in the lobby. Her pretty face glowed. She waggled some papers at him and came flying across the room talking so fast he couldn't understand her.

"It's out. The bills are already on the street and in three of the four banks I checked. I can tell for sure that the bills I found are not government printed, even though they are extremely well-done."

Spur caught her by the arm and pulled her into the corner of the lobby and quieted her down.

"Don't let the whole town know about it. Now what exactly have you found?"

She showed him five bills, all twenty-dollar denomination, and she fanned them out so he could see.

"The counterfeiters are spending the money already. The banks have it. I warned them but they can't be sure about the twenties. One bank won't take any twenty-dollar bill. Here's the bad part. Each of these counterfeit bills I found has a different serial number. I even found two that are in numerical sequence!"

"Oh, damn," Spur McCoy said. "Now we've got real trouble."

# Chapter Four

Clare Franks faced his father across the saddle of his horse. Clare had just returned from the small flag stop called Langtry, Texas, on the Southern Pacific Railroad and his father, Duncan Franks, was not at all pleased.

"What in hell is the trouble with you, boy? I send you to the railroad stop to pick up some salt licks and you're gone four days. What kind of a wild story are you gonna make up this time?"

"I had business in San Antonio that couldn't wait. Pa, I'm of age. I don't have to answer to you for every little thing I do."

Duncan Franks was six-foot-three with wide shoulders, a spade handle for a spine and the military bearing of a bird colonel, which was what he had been before he retired after serious wounds in the early Indian fighting.

His black hair belied his 52 years. He had come

to this part of central Texas ten years ago and had turned a barren hopeless homestead into one of the biggest cattle ranches in this part of the state. His granite-hard face shattered now and sagged into pain and frustration. "I'm counting on you, son. Why do you suppose that I've sweated my balls off in this wilderness to build up a ranch worth half-a-million dollars? Not to sell it to some Englishman and go live in Houston. I want you to carry on for me here. Get married and have six sons and teach them the cattle ranching business. You know that's my dream. You damn well better know that." He shook his head and took a deep breath. "You bring the salt licks back?"

"Yes, turned the wagon over to the foreman, Zeek, half a mile from the house and he's putting the licks where he needs them. Now I'd like to take a good hot bath and then have some supper and after that, a long night's sleep. I can use one."

"Clare, I want to know what you been doing for four days."

"I told you, Pa, that's my business. Just leave it alone. I got to have a life of my own."

"Hope to hell you ain't scribbling again. No man I know ever made a living trying to write them papers you keep working on."

"Mark Twain does nicely making a living writing."

"Who?"

"Mark Twain. He writes newspaper stories and novels and all sorts of things. He's traveled to Hawaii and Alaska and to California and all over."

"Well, you ain't Mark Twain. I just want you to tend to your business of learning how to run this ranch."

"Pa, I learned that when I was sixteen, can do it all blindfolded. All you have to do is hire the right men and delegate the jobs to be done. I need something a little more challenging."

"Like writing poetry I'd guess, like some namby-pamby little mother's boy who didn't never grow up into a man?"

"You still don't understand, Pa, do you? I want something more than a ranch. I want to write! I want to write a novel. I want to write the way Mark Twain does, write about anything, about everything. But first I'm going to need some money so I don't have to earn anything from my writing until I'm good enough."

"So stay with the ranch. Here is where your money will be coming from." Duncan looked at his son with a small glimmer of hope in his voice.

"I can't stay here forever. I need to travel, to see things, to go places, to meet new people."

"Like yesterday and three days before that when you were in San Antonio?"

"Yes, Pa, like that. Now I want that hot bath."

Clare left his father and went into the ranch house. It had seemed strangely silent these past two years after his mother died of the flu. The fever came suddenly and in two days she was gone. She understood about his writing. She encouraged him, helped him get more schooling.

Clarence Franks was small and slender, six inches shorter than his father, no more than 140 pounds, with a Van Dyke beard and long side burns. His soft brown hair was longer than most men's and he had bright blue eyes and a thin lipped mouth. He had wanted to be a writer since he finished high school that his mother had arranged for him by getting correspondence courses from the public schools of San Antonio.

His Pa would never understand a whit of what he felt about writing. Neither would the man Clare had ridden on the train with into San Antonio, but at least Henry Rhonstadt would be helpful in other ways. The raw potential was so great that Clare didn't even want to think about it.

Millions. All he wanted was maybe $50,000. That would keep him in comfort for several years and by that time he would be making his living by writing stories and novels. He had so many stories in his head. A lot of range and cattle and cowboy stories. That was all he knew, but he would expand his life and his contacts and his experiences to have other things to write about.

A real writer had to know something thoroughly to write about it. Women, yeah, even Holly would go in a book sometime. His very first. He had been as scared as she had been in the grass and tall weeds in back of Holly's house. But no one had seen them or interrupted them and it had happened.

Life! He had to experience life so he could write about it. He wondered how old Mark Twain was. Somebody said he was born in 1835 in Missouri. That would make him over 40. That was old. Twice as old as Clare.

Clare, short for Clarence. Yes, he'd change his name. Mark Twain had. He wondered what his writing name would be. But first the bath and then a big supper and three days at the ranch before he had to go back to San Antonio. Henry had said they should have some they could start passing by them. What a kick in the pants that would be.

He knew it was illegal and there was a small chance that he could go to prison. But he had to do it. He'd known Henry for years, and when Henry got the idea, they worked it out carefully. Of course they hadn't suspected that there would be anything so valuable in the Railway Express car. They had just figured on getting whatever was in the safe. It could be a huge payoff or almost nothing. That was part of the gamble. The registered mail had been a stroke of pure beginner's luck. No, not luck at all. It had been his destiny!

Destiny. This was how he would get a grub stake, a start so he didn't have to sweat out a living ten hours a day and then try to write. This way he'd have all day and half the night to write, wearing down hundreds of pencils and using up dozens of pen nibs to get the words exactly right.

Clare knew that he wasn't actually involved yet in anything illegal. He had taken no part in the train robbery. He told Henry that he was too well-known in Langtry. Clare showed them that his important part in the operation would come later when he took the train to other towns and opened bank accounts and then later wired to withdraw the money so he could get it in cash and later, in another town, he would deposit the legal tender bank notes in another bank. That way no one could trace the flow of the money, even if the first bank suspected something was wrong.

Oh, he would have to keep on the move for awhile, but then he would have his five years in Chicago or St. Louis or even New York or

New Orleans where he would dedicate himself to becoming another world famous writer.

Duncan Franks watched his only son walk away from the horse and go in the kitchen door. As usual, Clare had forgotten about the animal and left it for someone else to put away. The owner of the huge ranch waved at a cowboy near the corral who came for the horse.

This was a busy time. Bad weather had put off the spring roundup too long. They would be leaving in two days for the northern part of their range that stretched for miles into the rolling hills. Up in those small hills, there were a thousand places for cows and calves to hide.

Every hand would be needed, and Duncan was determined to have Clare along. It would do him good. He'd missed the last two roundups. Duncan needed to get the boy onto the range more, get a saddle under his pants and a rope in his hand and have him taste the dust and smell the burning skin and hair at the branding fire.

Clare was a good son but his soft and wonderful mother had coddled him too much, God rest her soul. Clare hadn't grown up quite the way Duncan wished he had. Now it was up to Duncan to finish the job. It might be a tough lesson, but a week long roundup would knock off some of the rough edges on the boy, and make him understand where he really belonged.

That is if Duncan himself could finish the roundup. Duncan had felt the twinges in his chest. He'd told the doctor about it and the old sawbone had told him it could be his heart and that he should slow down a little. But how in hell did an owner slow down when he had to be in on every roundup, every drive into San Antonio to the stock yards, when he had to plan out a breeding program to upgrade his stock and get another two-hundred brood cows to spark his herd?

That's why he had to have Clare trained totally in every aspect of the ranch operation from the books to the blood lines, to what brood stock to go after and what blooded bulls they needed for range breeding.

Managing a big ranch the right way was a tough, complicated, full-time job, and there was no place for foolishness such as this writing trash. A good week in the saddle would knock a lot of that writing enthusiasm out of Clare. It had worked before. It had to work again.

There was no way he could surprise Clare. He already knew about the roundup. Even on the off chance that he had forgotten, it would take all day tomorrow to get outfitted for the week in the field. The chuck wagon would be stocked, the crew would be working on the string of six ponies that each man needed for his work on the range.

That set Duncan to thinking about his own preparations. The chuck wagon was primary, else the crew wouldn't eat well and they'd have to slaughter a steer, instead of eating the dry food that every chuck wagon had. During the course of cutting out and throwing the yearlings, oftentimes one would get twisted around and break a neck or more likely a leg. Those were the animals that fell under the cook's quick skinning knife. There was something almost pagan about eating a steak from a steer that hadn't been properly blooded.

Usually it took ten to twelve hours for most of the blood to drain out of a butchered animal after it was slaughtered. Before that the flesh was overripe with blood and it gave the meat a wild, untamed, devilish kind of a taste that most of the men didn't enjoy.

Duncan rubbed his face. He had let his mind wander again. Hell, at 52 he was a long way from being used up, even on a ranch this size. He had 25 damn good years in his hide yet. But he'd just as soon turn over much of the running of the ranch to a younger man, his son, in say 10 or 12 years. The way things were going now, that didn't look like a good bet.

Duncan would talk to Clare tonight. The boy would have to understand. He'd use the "assumed sold" technique that a salesman in San Antonio told him about. With every customer, the salesman assumed that the person wanted to buy the product and that he had agreed to buy it. All they had to do was work out the cost of it, when it was to be delivered and exactly where the new owner lived.

Two days later they left on the roundup at five a.m. Clare growled a little but he was up and ready to go with the rest of the hands. The chuck wagon had been loaded and readied. The cook made them all a big breakfast; ham and eggs, flap jacks, bacon, toast, jam and coffee and they moved out on time.

The plan was to trail to the farthest edges of their ranch and work back toward the home place, gathering workable batches of cattle together in various locations, sorting them out, counting them, branding and cutting the new bull calves and branding the heifer calves.

The chuck wagon slowed them down. Twice they had to use extra horses to pull the rig out of bogs when crossing small creeks. They had 20 miles to cover to get to the spot where they would leave the chuck wagon and their remuda of spare cow ponies near a small spring. It took them all day to get there and it was after dark when they pulled the chuck wagon up to the spring and the cook began to warm up a huge pot of stew he had cooked the day before and carried along wrapped in a blanket and two chunks of ice from the ice house.

That night after they had eaten, Clare walked up to his father who had stretched out by the fire as the cool Texas night slid around them.

"Two more days, Pa. That's all I can spend out here. Then I've got business in San Antonio."

Duncan Franks looked up and scowled. He had been pleased the way Clare had helped with the wagon and became one of the crew.

"What's so all fired important that it can't wait a week?" Duncan asked.

"I have some business to get done. Depending how it goes, it could take me to Houston later on."

Duncan pushed the burned off ends of some sticks into the fire and blinked through a sudden gust of smoke. "Don't you think you should tell me what this new business is you have? If you need some financing, I can make you a loan."

"Pa, I told you before, this is my business and you don't need to be involved in no way. I want to do this on my own. You're always telling me to stand on my own two feet. This is one way I'm going to do it."

"You have enough money for this enterprise?"

Clare grinned. He dropped down beside the fire and sat there cross-legged, adding small branches to the blaze. "Oh, yes, Pa. In this operation, cash money is not any problem."

Duncan grunted, stirred the coals of the fire with a stick and looked up. "Clare, I've been around this old world a little longer than you have. I've seen it in operation in half the states in the Union. Believe me, money is always a problem. A few folks have too much. Most of us don't have enough. I still wish you'd tell me what you're doing. I hope it isn't some magazine you're trying to start, or a newspaper, or some other writing kind of business. Damn tough enterprises."

Clare laughed. "No, Pa. You can rest easy. I don't want to publish a magazine. Wouldn't mind writing for some of them, but that'll come later. Right now I'm ready to find my blankets. See you in the morning."

The next morning at sunup, the men had eaten a quick breakfast, gulped down scalding coffee and kicked their best roundup horses into motion. They divided the 12 men into two teams that rode four miles on west to the rims of some breaks. Then the teams each fanned out and began scouring the dips and ravines and flats, driving all the cattle they could find forward.

A mile out from the chuck wagon they had set up the branding fires. It was in an open space where they could bunch and hold the animals for cutting and sorting. They had been instructed to count the range bulls but not to gather them. The cows and calves and all of the steers were to get rounded up. They would be checked for any kind of disease and those with simple problems would be treated, counted and sent back to the range.

Clare worked the second group of six hands. He could ride as well as any of the cowboys. He was better with a rope than most of them. He flushed a cow and calf out of a small thicket and cut them off when the cow broke back the wrong direction. A few minutes later he had the mother and her calf walking sedately toward the rest of the gather they had bunched.

The lead man of the crew signalled the men about nine o'clock. They had over 60 head and he motioned for them to drive the animals the remaining mile to the smoke ahead that marked the branding fires.

There the real work began. Two men on cutting horses separated the calves and unbranded yearlings from the herd and a pair of ropers moved in. One hand threw a loop around the animal's head and rode forward slowly. The second cowboy used a sidearm cast of his lariat to slip his hoop under the caught animal's hind feet to make a heel catch.

Then the head catch cowboy rode ahead slowly and the heel catch man stopped. When the two ropes pulled tight, the animal's rear feet came together and it tipped over, falling to its side ready to be branded.

Clare was an expert as a heel roper and worked steadily until all of the unbranded calves and yearlings in the group had been finished. He watched the brander run up with his heavy leather gloves holding the three-foot long iron with its Bar F brand. The hand held the still glowing hot branding iron from the fire and pushed it hard against the animal's hip, holding it precisely long enough to burn through the hair and sear the skin but not burn all the way through the tough cowhide.

Branding was a hard job that took experience.

Clare had worked all summer one year to learn how to do it right. After that he taught the inexperienced hands how to brand.

Now he put in his hard day's work barely thinking about it. It was routine. Instead, he was thinking about doing a story concerning a young boy who was orphaned and loose on the Texas plains and had to make his own way when he was only 12 years old. What would the boy do? How would he survive? He began answering the questions, working out a general story that he could tell that would be interesting, exciting and might sell to a publisher.

Duncan Franks tried to be everywhere. He rode with one of the gather groups to get the roundup started, then supervised the branding and checked often with his tally man to be sure the was keeping an accurate record of every category of animal; bulls, cows, calves, yearlings and steers from two to four years old.

One team of three men cut out steers that were ready for market and held them in a bunch to one side. That group would be moved from one gathering spot to the next and by the time they had worked back to the home place, they would have a herd of market ready beef that would then soon be driven to San Antonio and the stock yards. There they would be sold to a cattle buyer who would sell a few locally, but most of them would be shipped by rail north to Chicago or toward the eastern markets.

Duncan rode his big palomino he had sent to Kentucky for. The stallion stood 16-hands and had a golden coat with almost a pure white mane and tail. He checked to the side and saw a market-ready steer surge out of the bunched herd heading west.

Duncan kicked his spurs into the palomino who charged after the steer. He swung his rope and caught up with the steer after 50 yards, roped it and tried to turn the heavy animal, but the steer wouldn't turn. It stopped and shook its head at Duncan, then took off west again away from the gather.

Duncan swore roundly and surged up on the animal again on its left side. He threw the line of his lasso around the right side of the steer so the rope belayed around its hind quarters.

The end of the lasso still held fast to the steer's head. Now Duncan angled away from the right side of the steer at a 45-degree point with his end of the lasso tight around his saddle horn with three dallies and a half hitch.

A few moments later the rope around the steer's hindquarters pulled tight, slid lower and neatly tripped the animal rolling it on its back.

The steer lay there a minute, brayed in anger and pain, then kicked around and scrambled to its feet and let itself be led gently back to the herd.

Later that same day another market-ready steer had bolted from the gather herd. When another hand had "busted" the steer with his rope the same way, the animal had broken a hind leg. It was quickly shot and the cook raced out to bleed the animal and rig a tripod of four-by-fours brought along for that very purpose.

The steer was hoisted to the top of the eight foot tripod, butchered out and left to drain. They'd have slightly blooded beef steaks for supper as soon as it was dark and the fourteen hour work day was over.

That afternoon, they made another sweep over at the far edges of their range. Duncan went with the gather team Clare was on this time.

The seven man group had just topped a small rise when Clare pointed ahead.

"Looks like we have visitors."

All the others saw them at the same time. Not a quarter of a mile away, four cowboys worked at gathering a herd of steers.

"Rustlers!" Duncan said. "They've got twenty-five head of market-ready beef. Let's go get them."

The men drew revolvers and charged forward. It was a minute or so before the rustlers realized they had been discovered. The two farthest riders turned and pounded hard away from the oncoming gunman. One man at the branding fire had to run for his horse and he was knocked down by a Colt .45 butt before he could get on his mount.

The fourth man mounted up but was ridden down and captured after a quarter mile run. The first two men got away clean.

Duncan sat on his big palomino and stared at the two men who stood facing him, hats gone, revolvers stripped from holsters, and hands already tied behind their backs.

"What in hell do you think you're doing here?" Duncan asked.

One man looked up and shook his head. "We hired on to some hombre in Langtry. Said he needed two more hands for a gather on his ranch. Said his name was Franks and he owned the Bar F. You mean he wasn't Duncan Franks?"

Duncan roared and swung his rope at the man who skittered back out of range.

"I'm Duncan Franks, you rustling bastard. Never seen a rustler yet who didn't have some wild assed story like that. You want to get hung or just shot to death?"

Clare stepped down from his mount and walked up to the other captive. The second one who had been at the fire looked to be about 17 years old. He was still a little shaken from being knocked down with the Colt butt to his head.

"What's your name?" Clare asked.

"Jimmy Jones."

"How old are you, Jimmy?"

"Sixteen and a half."

"You think the man who hired you was Duncan Franks?"

"Sure, he said he was. Why would anybody lie about it?"

"He'd lie to get you to come out here and help him rustle my cattle, that's why he'd lie. You're in big trouble, son. You know what we do with cattle rustlers in Texas?"

"No sir, I'm from Illinois."

"Don't apologize, you won't be going back there."

"Pa, we can take them into Judge Roy Bean, let him hold a court."

"Bean? Hell, that worthless, uneducated Mex killer ain't no kind of a judge. He's only a damned Justice of the Peace."

"He holds court, Pa, you know that. We let these two give us all the evidence and the judge decides."

Duncan turned his horse away from his son and stared around. A swale a half mile over showed a tall cottonwood tree. The ranch owner motioned.

"Over there, that cottonwood. Good as any. Put a lariat around their necks and we'll walk them over there. Don't matter none if they tire out. Last time they ever get tired. No sonsabitching rustlers are gonna get away with stealing my hard raised beef."

Clare turned and anger flared in his face. "Pa, you can't do this. The kid here is sixteen years old. You can't hang him. He thought he had a job as a cowboy. Can't you see that?"

"Don't matter none at'tal to me, Clare. He got caught rustling. Law says he hangs, so we save Roy Bean some trouble and the county some money. Let's move this pair over to that tree. Come on, we don't have all morning to waste. Let's get riding."

"Pa, you can't do this," Clare yelled where he stood near the youngest rustler. "I won't let you murder this poor kid."

"Won't, huh. How you plan on stopping us?"

Clare pulled the six-gun from his holster and eased back the hammer with his thumb. "This way, Pa. I'll shoot the first man who tries to put a noose around either of these men's heads. I mean it. I'll even shoot you, Pa, to stop you from murdering this young boy!"

# Chapter Five

In the lobby of the Drake Hotel in San Antonio, Spur McCoy grabbed at the five 20 dollar bills that Marci Philburton waved at him.

"That's right, Mr. McCoy. All five are counterfeit. All five were passed within the past two or three days. The bankers have no way of knowing just when. I found them in teller cash drawers and in some reserve money in the vault."

"I believe you. Let's go up to your room and take a closer look at them."

A few minutes later in Marci's room, she took out a kit from her luggage and produced a high power magnifying glass, some paper samples and several other devices and tools of her trade.

"The real paper is watermarked, of course, with a unique mark for the U.S. Treasury Department only. We won't find that watermark on this paper,

I can assure you. I can tell by the feel of the bills that they are fakes."

Spur took two of the bills and compared them. Identical, except for the serial numbers. Both different. He studied the bill again. It looked the same as a thousand others he had seen.

It was an 1875 series United States Treasury Note, legal tender for all debts both public and private. It was the usual sized note, with a picture of one of the presidents on the left side of the front in an oval. Directly below the picture was the serial number, seven digits and a letter. This one was A2811236 with a star at the end of the numbers. Earlier bills had only five serial numbers.

Earlier bank notes often had the number handwritten, but now all federal money had a printed serial number and the familiar green printed back from where the term "greenback" currency came.

He checked the rest of the note. *United States* was printed in large letters centered at the top of the bill in a curved fashion. To the far right stood some kind of a warrior woman holding a large white shield. Centering the bill was a large figure 20 against a reddish background circle seal. Below the circle was the written value of *Twenty Dollars*. At the very bottom in white lettering were the words *Treasury Note*.

He turned over the bill and found the familiar green reverse side with the regular three plaques. The two on each side held the denomination with the figure 20. These two were overlapped by a slightly larger plaque in the center that had a printed oval in the center that had the words *United States* at the top and *Of America* on the bottom. In the middle were a number of words and phrases printed in curious fashion of curved and slanted lines that Spur had never been able to understand.

He tossed the bills on the window sill where they stood in the daylight to examine them.

"How can you tell they're fakes? I never could."

"With practice, you could. It's the quality of the paper. The real stuff is made especially for us, has a bit of a cloth feel to it because it has a high rag content. That makes the bills last a lot longer. Regular paper would crumple and tear and wear out quickly.

"These fake bills also have good quality rag content paper, but there's a slight grain you can see in the paper making. Hard to catch but it's there. I can feel it when I smooth over a bill with my fingertips."

She held her magnifying glass over one of the bills on a lightly printed section and Spur nodded.

"Yeah, I can see the grain. Now show me a real bill so I can remember the difference. She took a good twenty dollar Treasury Note from her reticule and let him see the difference.

"Got it. On these counterfeits the serial numbers are all different, which means some mule is sitting by a press and printing one bill, changing the number of the bill in the form and printing another bill. He has to loosen the frame each time. That also means that these fake notes had to be run through the press three times. Once for the regular front of the bill from the engraving, and then a second time to print on the serial number of the bill in precisely the right location, then again for the back of the bill."

"Almost right. The press has to run again to put on the red seal under the large 20. Soon all the serial numbers on our printed currency will be in either red or green on each bill."

"Of course, green ink on the back. Now, how in hell do we find the people who are passing these?"

"We work with the banks. I've cautioned every bank in town to watch for the bills. They are Treasury Notes. You know there are several kinds of twenty-dollar bills in circulation. The Demand Twenty and the United States Notes. But neither of those has seven serial numbers."

"You going to be at one of the banks?"

"From now on. The minute a bill comes in with the seven digits, the teller is supposed to call me if I'm there or check with a supervisor. They take down the name and address of everyone who deposits or gets change for one of these Treasury Note bills."

"Then we hope we can tell which one came from which name."

"We'll know. The teller pins a slip of paper with the name and address of every customer passing one of the twenty Treasury Notes onto the bill. If I find any of them that are fake, we'll know where to follow up."

"Good, let's go check the banks and see what they've taken in so far."

It was a three hour bust. None of the banks had taken in any more of the twenty-dollar Treasury Notes.

"What now?" Marci asked. "Hey, come to think of it, we never did have dinner. It's after four. Are you ready for an early supper?"

He was. They ate at a small cafe that specialized

in steak and Spur enjoyed his meat and potatoes. She asked him what he'd learned that morning and at last he decided he could tell her.

"So you're going to put a watch on that house?"

"Sure as rhubarb in summertime. Soon as I get this steak defeated, I'm going out there."

"How can I help?"

"By getting a good night's sleep so you can check the banks in the morning."

Her lower lip pushed out in a pretend pout. "You won't let me help you?"

"You're being help enough. If we work both ends against the counterfeiters, we should be able to catch them."

"But I've never been on a house watch before. Please let me come. I won't get in the way."

"You'll be sitting on the ground behind a fence or a bush or something for hours. Still sound like lots of fun?"

"Yes. I can practice my star gazing. I'll recite the constellations for you starting with Taurus the bull, which might not be such a bad one to tell you about."

He relented. "Maybe. But don't even think about any kind of a romantic encounter out there in the dark. We can't afford to let this guy come and then vanish. It's through him I hope to find out who's doing the printing."

"I understand, and you don't have to be afraid of me. I'm not in the habit of raping grown men even if the moon is out and it's a romantic evening."

"Good. I'll hold you to that. Now, we still have three hours before dark. Let's get back to the hotel and change clothes. It's going to get on the chilly side before midnight."

"Midnight? We'll be out that long?"

"Probably. If you just passed three or four hundred dollars in fake bills, and got away with it, wouldn't you celebrate a little? My guess is that's what our counterfeiters are going to do. That will be my next stop. Trying to find a big spender at the gaming tables. How many gambling halls in town?"

She shook her head.

"I don't know either, but I may need to find out if our man doesn't come back to his rented house tonight. We can't count on them passing any more of the bills now that one bank won't take twenties anymore. They must know somebody is in town hunting them."

"That'll make it harder. But they might not know yet. I don't think they're going to the banks. They buy something with a twenty for fifty cents, throw away the goods and pocket the real nineteen-fifty. Lots of passing is done that way. It's slow, but it's the safest way."

"Not like they want to pass two thousand by putting it in their bank account."

"That's too risky for them. Oh, another thing about these bills. See how used they look? They've soiled them, wadded them up and smoothed them out. Made them to look like they're not brand new bills."

"Is that usual?"

"The good passers do that if they have time. Evidently this outfit has time. You find any printer that looked like he might be making money after hours?"

"No. I saw two of them. I hear there are two more in town. It must be one of them, but then again, they might have had a press freighted in from Houston and set up their own little print shop. They can afford to."

In their hotel rooms, they both took short naps. Marci changed clothes and Spur changed his shirt and put on a jacket to protect himself from the chill evening air. He double checked his six-gun and eased the hammer down on the empty cylinder.

When he knocked on Marci's door at seven that night, it was dusk.

By the time they walked the three blocks to the rental house, the sky was dark and filled with stars. They strolled past the house but it showed no lights. Spur looked around and went across the rutted path that served as the street to a house on the far side. It had no lights on either and in the side yard grew a pair of short bushy trees.

Spur stepped behind them and nodded.

"In here," he said. "No one from this house can see us, and if we part some of the lower branches, we can see across the street and the rented house. Good a spot as any."

Marci stepped into the spot and they broke off some inside branches of the deciduous tree, and tramped down a few more, then had a spot where they could sit down, still be hidden and see the suspect's house.

"How long do you guess?" Marci asked, pulling her sweater around her tighter.

"Can't tell. He might not come back at all tonight. That's why this isn't an easy job."

The wait began. They talked quietly about the case, but soon they ran out of even that. Marci dropped off to sleep for five minutes and awakened with a little cry.

"Oh, dear. I forgot where I was. I had this fine

little dream." She stopped and grinned. "I'll tell you about it later. Anything happen at our favorite house?"

"Not a thing yet. Quiet as a hundred year old tomb of an atheist."

"No resurrection, I get it. What do we do if he doesn't come back tonight?"

"We keep watching, we make a study of the eating places hunting a man with the description we have. Besides that, we hope to find somebody who can tell us who gave him the fake twenty."

By ten o'clock they both were cold, stiff and tired.

"Maybe you better get yourself back to the hotel," Spur said.

Marci peered out into the dark. "I'd have to go past three saloons to get to the hotel. I don't think I want to risk that alone. Women on the streets this late at night are not exactly safe."

"Agreed. So we'll wait a couple more hours if you can stand it."

"I'd need a little encouragement."

Spur reached over and kissed her lips. She clung to him a moment, then giggled.

"I hope the bad guy doesn't come right now."

She leaned in and kissed Spur again, her tongue stabbing at his closed mouth. Her hand reached for his crotch. She broke off the kiss and rubbed his fly.

"Remember that I'm one ahead of you, so I owe you one."

"Oh, yeah, I remember. Later tonight, maybe. Depending what our little friend out there does."

Nothing happened.

By midnight they both were getting fidgety.

"Let's call it a night and give it another try

tomorrow." They were so cramped and stiff that it took them a minute to stand and to get their legs working right. Then they walked slowly back to the hotel.

Marci caught his arm and marched in lock step with him as they worked down the street to the hotel. At the second saloon the swinging doors burst open and two men came out fighting each other. One punched the other so hard that the man fell to his hands and knees right in front of Spur and Marci. Spur guided her around the fallen man just in time for the other man to kick the downed combatant in the stomach, rolling him over on his back where he screamed and then vomited.

By that time they were past and almost to the hotel. They didn't check their key boxes, but went directly up to their rooms. She gave him her key and he unlocked the door and both went inside. Marci turned to him as soon as Spur closed the door.

"Now this is ever so much better than that hideout we had in the trees. Don't you think so?"

Spur caught her shoulders and pulled her tightly against him, then kissed her hard and demanding. He felt her go limp against him, then her knee lifted cautiously between his legs and massaged his inner thighs.

The kiss lasted a long time and when it ended she caught his hand and pulled him to the bed.

"Young man, you're seriously overdue and need some tender and loving attention. Sit down right here and we'll see what we can do to please you. Are there any requests?"

"I'd like the twenty-dollar special, the counterfeit twenty-dollar special."

"Sir, we just happen to have some of those specials in stock. First, we'll need to undress you to see if they fit properly. I'm sure you understand."

She took off his vest, then unbuttoned the fasteners on his shirt and played with the hair on his chest. Her fingers toyed with his man nipple, then she bent and sucked on the small button. His hands found her breasts. He held both and slowly massaged them, grinning as her breathing speeded up.

She moaned softly and ripped his shirt out of his pants and off his shoulders, then struggled with his belt. Spur undid the belt and opened the buttons on his fly, then turned the job back to her.

She pushed him on his back, straddled him and opened her blouse. She then removed it and lifted a silk chemise over her head so her breasts hung down.

"Have a late night snack to get your blood warmed up," she said. She lowered one breast into his mouth. Spur grinned and sucked in as much as he could, his tongue twanging her enlarged nipple and bringing soft little sounds from deep in her throat. She got one hand free and reached for his crotch where she worked through his short underwear and found his growing erection.

"Oh, yes, big boy, you're starting to grow. Get big and hard the way I love you best."

Spur pulled away from one of her breasts and moved to the other one, nibbling on the nipple, then licking it and at last sucking it into his mouth. She moaned and fell sideways on the bed. Her breath came in huge gasps and panting and her eyes were half closed as she kicked off her skirt and lifted to get out of her bloomers.

Marci spread her legs and lifted her knees.

"Darling Spur McCoy. Come make love to me right now. This very instant before I go crazy in the head from wanting you deep and hot and hard inside me. Hurry, before I explode and you'll never find more than small pieces of me spread all over this damn hotel room."

"You sure, woman? You're not just a cock tease, getting what you want and then putting me off the way you did last night?"

"Do I look like I'm putting you off?" She caught him by the arms and pulled him toward her. He chuckled.

"I always like to know that I'm wanted. Have to make sure you want to do this as much as I do."

"More, damn you, come on!"

He slid between her thighs and heard her sigh.

"Oh, yes, yes, hurry."

She pulled down his shorts so his erection sprang out and cooed a moment at the sight, then grabbed him and pulled him toward her crotch. He slid forward and a moment later she felt the first penetration.

"Oh, lord, yes, that's the place. Push in."

Spur smiled and thrust hard with his hips as he plunged into her deeply until his pelvic bones hit hers and she yelped in approval.

At once he felt her legs lift and circle his waist and lock together. The new angle gave him another inch of penetration and she squealed as he pressed in deeper.

"Oh, damn, oh damn, oh damn, this is so fine. So damn wonderful and fine and beautiful. I love it, I just love it. I don't see why I don't get married and get this every night for the rest of my life." She blinked and looked at him. "No, maybe not every night, more like two or three times a night. Yeah!"

Spur thrust gently and at a slow pace until she began to meet his hips with her own.

"Faster, faster, I want to see some action out of you."

Spur chuckled and worked faster. He could sense her passion building again, then his own shot to the front and he knew he was close but he had no intention of stopping it.

Before he knew it was there, he exploded into a billion particles, spraying the whole town, jetting into the sky as his hips pounded again and again and his breathing stopped until he thought he would die from lack of air.

Then he felt her hips pounding upward and her whole body stiffened as she spasmed and vibrated and let out a low moaning cry that harkened back to the primitive drives of the species in the eons-old ritual of the reproduction process.

He gasped and sucked in enough air to live on as she kept on climaxing for another minute and then gave a large sigh and relaxed. Her breathing slowed until she was back to normal.

"Oh, God, how beautiful," she whispered, not ready yet to let go of the wonder and rapture of the moment, feasting on it and making it last as long as she could.

After what seemed to Spur like ten minutes,

Marci opened her eyes, highlighting a smile such as he hadn't seen in years. It was pure joy and sheer beauty.

"So wonderful. You're wonderful. Who said a woman would do anything for a man just after he'd made love to her? Whoever said it was right. At this second I'd kill for you, Spur McCoy. Just point him or her out and give me a shotgun so I can't miss and I'll blast anyone you want me to."

"I'll make up a list. Right on top I want the two men who robbed that train."

"Easy, but that'll have to wait until tomorrow." She frowned and moved her hips as he came away from her and lay beside her on the bed.

"That makes me wonder if the mysterious renter has gone back to his house. How will we know?" Marci asked.

"We won't unless he stays for a while. I'll be out to his place about six in the morning to see if he was, or is, there and track him when he leaves. Now that we know some of the bills are in circulation, it means they're ahead of where we thought they might be. They set up their printing operation quickly."

"Why only five bills have shown up?"

"I'd say it was a test, to see how easy it was to pass the bills to merchants. The next time they may try a bank. The trouble is it might not be one here in town."

"Where? Houston, Austin?"

"Austin would be closer. The train runs up there. It's only about eighty-five miles away, three hours by train. I might send you up there to talk to the banks. Let's see what happens tomorrow."

He rolled toward her and kissed her. "Now how

about some sleep? I want to get out of my boots and my pants. Hope you don't mind. Shall I stay here or go back to my room?"

"You mean to sleep?"

He nodded.

"Sure, sleep here. I promise not to seduce you in your dreamland time, but I do get to snuggle up against you. Been a long time since I've gone to sleep pushed up tight to a gorgeous hunk of man in my bed."

"Good, I can use the shut-eye time. I'll try not to wake you up when I roll out in the morning."

"You do and I'll be mad as a mama hornet with a nest full of young ones. Wake me up for a quick goodbye."

"We'll see."

"Hey, McCoy. Are we going to catch these guys?"

"Damn right, Philburton. We'll grab them all and get the plates back. You can count on that."

He had stripped off his pants and his boots and she pulled down his short underwear.

"We both should sleep nude tonight, that's the healthiest way," she said.

He frowned.

"Come on try it, you might find it interesting."

# Chapter Six

Marci awoke the next morning alone in her bed. She scowled, stretched and struggled out from the sheets just before eight o'clock. She was not an early morning person. Marci smiled when she realized she was still naked. It had been so reassuring last night simply going to sleep beside the warm body of a nice man.

Spur McCoy was a good man. Thoughtful, kind, considerate and also bull-headed and hard to get along with. She smiled again. But the other benefits of working with him were enormously satisfying. She felt a little soreness deep down between her legs.

About time. She hadn't been sore in that spot for at least a year. It made her smile again.

An hour later she started her tours of the banks. It was the third bank she checked where she found another Treasury Note that had the same general sequence of serial numbers. They had changed only the last two digits up to the first 99, then probably would go to the 100's for the next change. The first four numbers on all the bills were the same. That helped to find them.

She guessed that on the next printing they would change the first four numbers as well—if there was another printing. For all she knew, they might have been running a press day and night and turned out a million dollars worth so far. How many bills would that be? She tried to think of the number, but got mixed up in her division and gave up.

The new counterfeit she found had a note pinned on it saying that the bill had been turned in by Adolph Carter, from the San Antonio General Merchandise store. She reported it to the bank manager, who debited that account, and she signed a receipt for the fake note. Then she took the bill and walked down four blocks to the big store. A sign over the door bragged that this was the first store in San Antonio and the oldest retail operation in town.

Inside she talked to a gentle man in his fifties who looked shocked when she told him he had passed a worthless counterfeit twenty-dollar bill to the bank.

"I've seen some bad bills in my time, but not lately," he said spreading his hands wide. "I didn't mean to pass on a counterfeit, believe me."

Marci told him she didn't blame him. "These bills are almost perfect. Only an expert can pick them out." She showed him the bill and he said it still looked good to him. She explained the only difference was the quality of the paper and he seemed satisfied.

"There is no way anyone but a trained person could pick out these counterfeits," she told him. "Oh, you might want to write down the serial number. If you find any bills with these first four serial numbers, chances are you have another fake bill."

He wrote down the numbers and put it on the counter near his cash drawer.

"Now, do you know who gave you that twenty?"

"Oh, yes indeed. Young man gave it to me last evening just before closing. Bought food with it, mostly only two dollars change as I recall."

"How do you know he was the one?"

"A twenty-dollar bill is half a month's pay for most town folks, near a month's wages for a cowboy. Most folks don't use the twenties or fifties or hundreds. Most are lucky to get ahold of a five-dollar bill. Fact is, I took in only one twenty-dollar bill all day yesterday, and it was from this young man."

"Good. That's the kind of evidence and proof we're looking for. Now, do you know the man's name, or can you describe him for me?"

"You bet, on the description. Looked kind of like my nephew, that's why I remember. He was maybe twenty or a year older. Clean shaven, nearly six feet tall, tanned face and had green eyes, just like Billy. From the way he talked I'd say he came from the east around Boston somewhere not too long ago. The more time them easterners live out here, the more of their accent they lose."

"Fat or thin? How was he dressed?"

"Thin like a well weathered Texas fence post. Wore town clothes, dark pants, white shirt, a dark vest, and a coat that didn't quite match his pants."

"Did he seem in a hurry, nervous, jittery?"

"Calm as a well fed cow chewing her cud."

Marci dug into her purse and brought out a real twenty-dollar bill. "We're not supposed to do this, but the bank reduced your account by twenty dollars when we confiscated the bill. So here's a good twenty to replace it." She smiled at the surprise on the merchant's face.

"You keep watching now for any bills with those first four serial numbers. If that same man comes back in, try and find out his name and where he lives. We'd appreciate it." She shook his hand and hurried out the door, anxious to tell Spur what she had found.

Five blocks down the street, Spur McCoy watched the house where he suspected the man who bought the 60-percent dynamite and could be the train robber lived. He'd been there behind the bush since six a.m. There had been no light and no smoke from the small house.

About eight, a man came out of the house right beside Spur, but missed spotting Spur in his bushy tree and went down the street evidently to work.

By ten that morning, Spur gave up his watch on the suspect's house. The man either wasn't there or had left before Spur arrived. It could be that he was not the one involved at all.

Spur walked back to the Drake Hotel and had just settled down to a cup of coffee and a cinnamon roll in the dining room when Marci hurried up to his table and sat down, her eyes serious and sparkling bright.

"Had another bill passed yesterday, turned in today. It came from the General Store and I got a description of the man." She gave Spur the description.

"Think he's the same one who might be at the house and who bought the dynamite?"

"The descriptions sound a lot alike. He could have shaved off the beard and left his wig at home this time. He sure doesn't spend much time at that rented house."

"How can we find him? There must be five or six thousand people in San Antonio by now."

"Makes it tougher than if it was out in Langtry where the robbery took place."

"Would it do us any good to ride out there on the train and see what we could find out?"

"We could talk to Judge Roy Bean, but he was on the other side of the train, didn't see anything until the robbers took off at a gallop into the dry Texas outback country," Spur said.

"We've got to do something."

"Marci, you keep watching the banks until they've counted all the money they took in today. There might be another twenty we could get some more information about. I'm going to check on those other two printers I didn't get to before. I might strike pay dirt at either one."

She had ordered coffee and nibbled on the edge of his roll. They both finished their coffee and went outside.

"Maybe I should come with you to the printers. I could distract them while you looked around."

"Not that complicated. Better use of our time for you to check on those twenties."

She pouted a minute, then shrugged and gave him a short hug and hurried down the street. Spur stood there a moment admiring the smooth way her hips worked under the tight tan skirt. He grinned thinking how well those same hips worked all bare ass naked in his bed pounding upward against him.

He shook his head and found the fourth printer. The place was on a side street in an old wooden building. A fire just asking to happen.

The pristine clean press stood on a metal floor plate a dozen feet from the front door. It's non-moving parts had been painted in some bright sequence and the working sections looked clean and well oiled.

A man well into his sixties looked up, pushed a green eyeshade back on his forehead and grinned.

"What the hell can I do for you today, young feller?"

Spur had to smile in spite of himself. If this man was a counterfeiter, he was also the best actor this side of the Allegheny.

"Looking to find myself a printer. Are you any good?"

The older man chuckled. "Good? I just ruined three of them damn diplomas. Wished to hell I hadn't said I'd do them. It's a free job, of course, for the Sunday School. Good? Damn, I don't know. Right now I feel about as useless as balls on a heifer."

Spur laughed and finished his rapid visual inspection of the 20 by 40 foot building. Nowhere to hide a counterfeit operation in here. Besides, the place was as neat as the inside of a virgin's corset. Not a piece of paper on the floor, no stacks of salvaged paper, no pads, no open boxes of paper getting dusty.

McCoy nodded at the old man. "If I do pick you as my printer it won't be boring. Thanks for the look-around. I just might be back to see you with some paying business."

Spur waved and the eyeshade came back down on the printer as he bent to his pro bono task of getting the Sunday School certificates printed.

It took Spur a half hour to find the last printer. Two people he asked had never heard of the shop. Three more gave him directions and at last he spotted the small place crowded between a leather goods and saddlery store, and a boot and shoe store.

Inside, the print shop looked even smaller. The place was only 12 feet wide and 40 feet long. A woman at a counter across the front of the store watched him come in.

"What's yours today?" she asked.

He wanted to say a draft beer, but he controlled himself and asked about printing up some business cards. The woman turned and shouted at the man in back.

It would take a week she told him. Her husband was way behind in his work. The place was only semi neat and clean. A tarp covered a press toward the back and there was a big supply of paper in all sizes and colors stacked along the wall. It was a possibility for a night-time work spot.

He got a quote from the woman on the business cards, and left saying he'd be back when he got an address tied down. She nodded and he hurried out the door.

On his way back to the hotel, Spur passed the San Antonio General Merchandise Store. He decided to stop in and see if the merchant remembered anything else about the man who had given him the twenty-dollar bill.

He headed for the counter near the back of the store when a familiar voice called to him. "McCoy, get back here, we've got some good news."

It was Marci. She popped up from behind the horse collars and grinned at him.

"The same guy came back to get some food items he'd forgotten before and Mr. Herrick got him talking. Mr. Herrick says he likes to know about his customers, their names and where they live in case he has to deliver some food sometime.

"Anyway, the guy was friendly enough, talked, said his name was O.J. Nathan and that he lived at that same address that we have for the dynamite man."

Spur grinned and kissed Marci on the cheek. "Good work, Marci. Now we're getting somewhere. How long ago was this Nathan here?"

"It's been nearly an hour now. From what he bought, Mr. Herrick said that Nathan could be doing some baking."

"Let's go. He might still be at home."

They thanked the store owner and hurried out the front door and down the street toward the small house they had watched before. This time they didn't hide or watch, they walked up to the front door and Spur knocked on the painted wood.

No one responded.

Spur knocked again, longer, louder. Still there was no answer. They left and walked to the end of the block, went down the intersecting street that had only one house on it and along the street in back of the suspect's place.

"You just keep on going," Spur told Marci. "I'm going to see if this guy locks his doors and if he has anything to hide inside, like a couple of hundred thousand in twenty-dollar bills."

"I want to come."

"No. Too dangerous. Somebody would see two of us slipping into his place ten times as easily as they would just one. Now scoot. I'll meet you back in the lobby at the Drake just as soon as I get through in here."

"You never let me have any fun," she said, a frown developing into a pout.

"I thought we had lots of fun last night," Spur said. Marci grinned, lifted her brows and walked away down the rutted dirt path that passed for an ungraded street.

Spur walked down the street behind her until he was in back of the target house. He turned and as if he belonged there, he walked up to the back door of the place, twisted the knob and went inside.

He entered a small back porch that held a rick of wood and an ancient wooden tub and a washboard. He saw another door beyond. At the door, Spur listened intently but could hear no one inside. He turned the knob and the door opened. He pushed it in gently. When he had it open far enough to slip inside, he edged through the opening and looked around.

The kitchen. Two paper sacks filled with something sat on the table. He checked and found grocery staples, bread and some bacon that showed out the top.

In the next room, he looked at the furniture. Evidently, the place came ready to live in with dishes and linens and all. A few papers scattered on a dining room table. They made no sense to him. One was about a train excursion to San Francisco. Another about the price of horses in Wyoming. A third handwritten one that was most interesting.

Figures on the sheet of tablet paper divided $50,000 into three parts coming up with $17,000, which wasn't right. A three way split on the counterfeit loot? That would take 2,500 of the twenty-dollar bills. Could be done with time. At least it looked like the man who lived here was tied to the counterfeiting.

Spur knew he should have two people watching this house around the clock, both front and back doors. He pounded his fist on the table. All the time he had been watching the front door, this guy could have been coming and going by the back door.

So, there must be a tie between this guy and the robbery and the subsequent printing of the bills. But who was doing the printing? He had to take another run at the printers. At night still was the best time to catch them. That's when they would be running the presses, cutting out the bills and then messing up the finished notes so they looked used.

He went through the four room house quickly, staying away from the unshuttered windows. There was a bed that had been slept in. The kitchen had been used. The wood range was cold. A supply of wood filled a box nearby. A new fire had been laid in the cook stove.

Nothing else. No box filled with counterfeits. No locked bag with the engraved plates in it.

Spur took one last look and went out of the kitchen into the small back porch. He stared out the screen on the door, saw nobody in the area, so stepped through the door, closed it and walked to the next street behind the house and strode toward the downtown section.

The printer was the key. He had to strike fast

before the counterfeit gang moved out of town. If he was running this operation, he'd have printed the paper here, rushed it to the train and hit Austin or Houston before he passed any. Get away from the scene. He just hoped these counterfeiters were beginners.

They had chanced on the plates, Spur was fairly certain of that. Whoever robbed the train knew how valuable the plates where and hit the first town big enough to have a printer.

That still didn't get the identity of the printing man. Who the hell was he? Spur felt that he had talked to the culprit in his rounds of the five establishments, but he hadn't the slightest idea of which one it might be. He could count out one or two, but on the other hand, those might be the exact ones to suspect the most.

Food. He always thought best on a full stomach. He'd find Marci at the hotel and arrange for a good lunch. . . . no, damnit, a good dinner. By then he'd have an idea. By then he damn well better have a good idea.

# Chapter Seven

Several days before Spur McCoy arrived in San Antonio, Clare Franks stood on a dusty stretch of country 15 miles from Langtry, Texas, holding his six-gun loosely covering his own father and three of the cowboys on the gather.

"I mean it, Pa. You try to hang this kid and I'll shoot sure as all hell. You want to take the chance?"

His father astride the big palomino stallion laughed. "Time you shoot me is when hell freezes over, kid. You ain't got the smarts, you ain't got the nerve, and besides that, you handle that hog leg like an old woman. Now, Parker!"

Duncan Franks barked the order and Clare looked to his right, then back to his left. He had just begun to turn when a man galloped up behind him, dove off his horse like he was bulldogging a steer and smashed Clare to the ground. The six-gun fired but the round drilled into the ground a dozen feet from anyone.

The rider named Parker kicked the weapon out of Clare's hand and pulled the younger and smaller man to his feet.

"That's enough, Parker. Get your horse and help us take these two buzzard baits over to that cottonwood. About time all of you get a hard-assed lesson in just what it takes to build a ranch in this godforsaken country. Move it now!"

Lariats furled out, the two rustlers had the loops settled around their necks, then were led toward the cottonwood. Parker picked up Clare's .44 and tossed it to Duncan Franks who pushed it in his own belt.

Duncan stared at Clare who stood where Parker had left him.

"Get on your mount, boy, and I'll show you that it takes some guts to be a rancher. Move it!"

"You're not a colonel now, Pa. I don't have to do things just because you say so."

The shot came as a jolting surprise to Clare who jumped sideways as the .45 round tore into the sod beside his left foot. He looked back at his father.

"All those years growing up I thought I knew you, Pa, but I can see now that I never did. You were always the colonel, and I had to do what a colonel told me to do. No more. Go ahead, shoot me. That's the only way you can stop me. I'm going to report you to Judge Roy Bean if you hang those two boys."

"He'll laugh you out of his saloon, boy, you should know that. Now get on your horse and come along. You just ain't got no choices left.

You walk or ride out of here and you go without a dime of my money, you know that?"

"I don't want your dirty money."

"It's not dirty money. It's hard worked for, tough earned, honest cash. I'm building up this ranch for you, Clarence, don't you understand that for God's sakes?"

"You're building it up for you, Pa, so you can say you have the biggest spread in this part of Texas."

"You gonna mount up, boy, or you want to walk?"

Clare nodded. "Oh, I'll ride, ride right into town and go all the way to San Antonio and the sheriff if I have to. Judge Bean hasn't any jurisdiction over a hanging, anyway. I should have thought of that."

Clare mounted and looked back at his father. "You just bluffing about hanging them to scare the two? That what you're doing?"

"Sure boy, sure. That's it. Rope around their necks but the end of the line won't be tied off at the tree. Scare the shit right out of them."

"That I can live with," Clare said. He kicked his horse into motion and headed for the men ahead who had almost reached the cottonwood.

Duncan himself saw to the nooses and the tie off on the big cottonwood. The limb selected came only four feet from the trunk of the big tree, but Duncan said it was enough. They'd hang the older one first, then the younger one.

Clare would have nothing to do with the preparations. He watched silently as the older of the two was hoisted onto one of the horses. The man faced backwards on the mount near his rump. Another horseman put the noose around the man's throat. Clare knew that the noose wouldn't break the man's neck the way a thick, heavy looped rope would. So the man would strangle to death.

Clare nodded. Except his Pa said the rope wouldn't be tied off. The rustler would be jolted off the horse, hit the end of the rope and scream and think he was about to be hung, but the rope would pull away from the tree limb overhead and he would fall to the ground bruised a little but relatively unhurt.

Scare the hell out of them.

Duncan rode over and blindfolded the seventeen-year old so he couldn't see what was about to happen to the other man they were hanging.

"Ready?" Duncan called. The man at the tree and the man holding the horse with the rustler on board sang out that they were.

Duncan rode up to Clare. "Son, I want you to whip the horse out from under the rustler. Do it right."

Clare wanted to refuse, but he had his father's word that the man wouldn't die. It would be all right.

He stared at his father. "The rope isn't tied off at the tree?"

"No, it's like I told you. Go check it yourself if you want to."

Clare frowned, shrugged and rode up to the black where the rustler sat. Clare stared into the man's eyes a moment.

"Don't worry," he said softly so no one else could hear. Then he used his reins and slapped the black hard on the rump. He hit the mount twice, then she surged ahead and the rustler slid off the black's rear quarters and dropped.

Clare held his breath. Then from four feet away he stared in horror as the rope held.

It had been tied off!

Clare pulled a sheath knife from his belt and kicked his mount up to the hanging man and slashed twice at the rope. The thin rope cut through and the rustler fell hard to the ground.

Clare dropped off his horse holding the knife. He pulled the noose away from the man's throat and saw him cough and gag and then begin to breathe again.

Clare stood, turned in a slow circle and brandished the six-inch razor bladed knife.

"Any of you come near me or this man, I'll slash you to bits," he screamed. "Don't make a mistake, I mean it. You want to stop me, shoot me dead right here. I won't let you murder this man or the kid." He waited a minute, then stared at the three hired men. "Parker, Ling, Southfield. Get the hell out of here and go get that next gather started. The rest of you move out, get away from here before I come after you and cut your legs right off your stirrups!"

Parker grinned, turned his mount and rode off toward the far section of the Bar F range where the gather would continue. Three of the other riders saw his lead and followed. The last two men looked at Duncan. He waved them away.

Left at the cottonwood were Clare and his father, still mounted, and the two accidental rustlers. Clare cut their hands loose and pointed the knife at them.

"You two, you came about as close as a man can come to getting hanged today. Do you understand about that?"

The kid nodded. The older hand had recovered.

Tears surged up in his eyes and he knelt in front of Clare.

"Thanks for saving my hide. Won't never take a job on a spread unless I ride through the home place ranch buildings first and make sure it's a legitimate outfit."

Clare looked at the seventeen-year old. He nodded. Clare had taken the blindfold off him.

"Yeah, me too. Damn, I figured it was a real job."

"Next time make sure who you're working for. Now, both of you, sit down and take your boots and socks off."

"Oh, damn," the older hand said.

They did. Clare had them tie the laces together, then he looped them around his saddle horn.

"Walk," Clare said.

"Which way?" the kid asked.

"Follow me," the older hand said. "Right now anywhere away from here is the right direction."

"Oh, damn that hurts," the kid said stepping tenderly on bare feet as he followed the older cowboy across the Texas outback.

Duncan Franks had sat his horse and watched. He kicked the stallion into motion and rode up beside Clare. Duncan still wore a grin of surprise and pleasure on his rugged tanned face.

"I'll be good God damned and flipped sideways if it didn't work out just about right."

Clare whirled, anger clouding his face.

"If I'd let you have your way, you'd have hung that man."

Duncan grinned. "That what you think?"

"You did have me slap the horse away. But you said the rope was not tied off."

"Wasn't at first, then I had this better idea."

Clare scowled. "You had a better. . . ." He sighed. "So you figured there was no way that I would let the man die. I could haul him up on my horse or cut the rope."

"Me, I figured that?" Duncan said grinning. "Now, cowboy. I think it's time that we get moving so we can get another gather in before we waste the whole fucking day."

Clare worked the two days on the roundup, roping and branding, the way he told his father he would. The night of the second day, he walked over to his father near the chuck wagon.

"Pa, like I told you. I put in my two days out here. Now I have to go to San Antonio."

"This about some woman?"

Clare grinned. "No, Pa, no woman. Just something that I have to do."

"When will you be back?"

"Not sure, maybe a few days. Maybe a few weeks. I'll just see how it goes."

"Don't make me unhappy, Clare, with whatever you do. I don't know what you're going to try in San Antonio. However, I did learn something about you today. With those rustlers, you were fair, and at the same time tough. You ever walked through this country for twenty miles with no boots or socks?"

"Won't be so bad. By the time they got out of sight of us, they should have cut up their hats and made covers for their feet. Least that's what I figured they'd do. Been done before."

Duncan nodded. "You need any cash?"

"Got me a couple of dollars, Pa."

"The ranch is here waiting for you when you get back. Might work out for you to write some of them stories here for a time. Kind of do both jobs and still have a full belly and a place to sleep. Could beat being broke and hungry in Austin or Houston."

Clare considered that. "I'll think on it, Pa."

Clare rode to the Bar F home place and stayed the night. The next morning he packed a small bag and rode into the flag stop of Langtry. It was one stop where the flag was out for every train.

Before noon Clare landed in San Antonio, started to register at a hotel, then changed his mind and walked down the street looking at the names of business firms. He had to go several blocks before he saw the name of the printer he searched for. Clare went around to the back door and slipped inside.

A man with bushy black hair, spectacles and ink smeared on his printer's apron looked up, surprise on his stubbled face.

"I'm Clare Franks. I'm supposed to meet a man here named Henry Rhonstadt."

The printer's frown vanished. "Good, good. We're at the point now where we need another face that isn't so well-known in our town. Welcome to our little enterprise."

"Where's Henry?"

"He's out buying some more food from a different store. Figures we all better just stay right here in the print shop until we're ready to get on the train."

Clare's face clouded, his eyes narrowed. "Don't remember nothing about a train ride just yet. You have it all printed?"

The older man shook his head. He worked at a press wiping black ink off a roller, getting it ready to put on a second color.

"Wrong as rhubarb in July, boy. It's a long job

printing up those bills with a new number on each one. Takes one hell of a long time. Should get done tonight with you to help us."

"Can I see some of it, some of the money? I've seen the plates but not much more. I had some ranching I had to do a few days."

"I heard tell." The printer wiped his inky hands on a rag and reached in the pocket of his dark blue printer's apron that was by now nearly black with ink. He took out a twenty-dollar bill that had been folded twice and handed it to Clare.

"There 'tis, fresh and pretty and smudged up some so it don't look so damn new. Part of the job we need doing, messing up them bills so we can pass them easier. Oh, they call me Jennings, Osgood Jennings." He held out his hand, ink and all, and Clare took it with a firm grip.

"Pleased to meet you, Mr. Jennings. What day is this?"

"Day? Glory, who cares?" He looked at a calendar on the wall. "Peers to be Thursday, May 22."

"Good. This is the day I promised Henry I'd be here to help with the printing and the passing." He unfolded the twenty-dollar bill and studied it. "Dang me if it don't look real. Just as clear and pretty as them you get straight from the bank."

"Damn right. Top notch quality print job, did that myself. If I'd had the same paper the Bureau uses back in Washington, they never would have been able to track these bills."

"Paper seems the same to me," Clare said.

Osgood Jennings chuckled. "Good. That's what most folks is gonna say. We don't get into the other room where the good press is until Henry comes back. I give him the key. She's locked up tighter than an old maid schoolmarm with a corset." Jennings cackled at his own joke and motioned to Clare.

"Might as well make yourself useful around here. I've got two jobs to get finished for good friends before I take my long awaited vacation."

Jennings put Clare to work boxing up some finished printing and cleaning up the work table.

An hour later Henry Rhonstadt came back and he waved at Clare.

"Hey, cowboy, good to see you. Figured as how you might have bayed at the moon once too often and decided not to come with us."

"Not me, Henry. I'm in for the ride. Hell, I got myself fed up with ranching and working them damned cows. You know that. We talked about it enough when I went in to drink with you at Langtry."

"That you did." Henry took off a long hair wig and a paste on moustache and put them to one side. "Let's get this print job finished up." He moved toward the locked door Clare had seen before.

"I'll lock up the front door and put out the closed sign," Jennings said. "No sense taking any chances."

Clare went with Henry who opened the padlock and swung back the door. Henry found a coal oil lamp near the door and lit the wick, then lit three more and hung two over the press in the windowless room that was 10 feet wide and 12 long.

Clare looked at the press with wonder. It was the most marvelous machine he'd ever seen. The working parts were painted three different colors, reds and greens and black, evidently depending on their function.

The round platen was shiny and smooth and the ink rollers poised and ready over the form that held in the twenty-dollar-bill engraving.

A work table just beyond the press held stacks of printed paper that looked to be four by eight inches. Since there was just one engraved plate, only one bill could be printed at a time.

"Takes one press run on the back of the bills, then another run on the face," Henry explained. "After that we have to print in the red seal and the serial number in red ink on the front of the bills. Three runs through the press and the registration of the paper must be exactly right or the bills won't have a chance of passing."

"A lot of work," Clare said.

Henry shrugged. "Be worth it. We've already passed more than two hundred dollars worth here in town. Haven't heard a yelp by anybody yet, so I guess nobody knows that we're here."

"What can I do to help?" Clare asked.

"Right back here, buddy. You can make these nice new twenty-dollar Treasury Notes look like they are old and much used. Want you to take each bill and rub it in this pan of dirt, then crinkle up each bill into a ball and spread it out flat again. By that time the bill looks like it's been in a hundred wallets."

"Seems a shame to mess up such good press work," Clare said.

"Yeah, but that's the only way we can be sure to pass them. We don't want some store owner getting fussy about the twenties that he takes in."

Clare picked up a stack of the bills that had

been trimmed down to their regular size, three and one-eighth inches wide and seven and three-eighth inches long.

"Careful, Clare, that's nigh on to a thousand dollars worth of Treasury Notes you're holding."

Clare looked at them in awe, then put the stack down and took them one by one. He "weathered" them the way he had been told. At first it was exciting, but after 20, or $400 worth, it got boring. The fun would come in passing the money.

Clare watched the press operation. The paper was put in exactly right; then the press ran through one rotation. That printed bill was taken off and laid on the table for the ink to dry. The pressman checked the ink, put another piece of paper firmly between posts that gave it the proper position or register as the printers said and rolled the press again.

Each time they made $20. That was a lot faster than raising a bawling calf for four years so it could be driven to market and sold for $30 or $40. Of course, the money had to be passed first.

Clare worked three hours until his back and shoulders ached. He looked up and saw the other two men cleaning their hands.

"Supper time," Henry said. "I brought back some bread and cheese and a half gallon of milk. Best we can do tonight. We'll eat high on the hog in just a week or so."

During the meal, the other two men had a small argument and Clare listened closely.

"Don't care," Jennings said. "Figure we should get it all printed up first before we take any big chances."

"Won't be a big chance. In Austin the banks get so busy that they won't even notice a thousand dollar deposit. Figure now that we have Clare, we'll both go up to Austin first thing in the morning on the train, make the deposits in two banks and be back here before dark."

"Don't like it. Too many things to go wrong."

"Won't, Jennings." Henry fingered the six-gun he had pushed into his belt. He caressed the wooden handle and looked back at Jennings. "Remember who's the boss around here. Only reason I let you do the printing was because I knew you've done some prison time. You won't go running to the sheriff. You do the printing and I'll handle the rest of it and you get your share."

"How do we get the money out of the bank?" Jennings asked.

"Simple. We go to Houston and tell the bank there we have an account in Austin and need nine hundred and fifty dollars. The bank there sends a wire to the Austin bank requesting the withdrawal. The Austin bank makes the withdrawal and wires the money to the bank in Houston. Best part is that the cash we pick up in Houston is genuine U.S. currency. We washed that bad money and made it pristine clean again."

Jennings finished chewing his bite of cheese sandwich and nodded. "If'n you say so. We'll have a secret account number or some such?"

"Depends on the bank. It works. I've done it before on a small scale. Don't worry about that."

They finished eating and went back to work.

"We got to have two thousand dollars worth ready to go by morning," Henry said.

Jennings nodded. "We got 150 bills all done and printed with a different serial number on each one. Now it's up to Clare over there to get them messed up enough so you can pass them."

Clare grinned. "I'll be ready. I just hope that we take along a couple of spares we can spend while we're in Austin. I ain't never been in the state capital before."

Henry grinned. "Yeah, we'll do that. You do good in the big city and I might treat you to a session in the best cathouse this side of Houston."

Clare wadded up two twenty-dollar bills at once and grinned at the mention of the house of ill repute. There was something else to look forward to. He'd never been to a whorehouse either.

# Chapter Eight

Spur McCoy had his good noon meal with Marci. She was bubbling over with high expectations.

"So I asked the bank teller who passed the bill and he said it came from a friend of his, Ed Martin. He was surprised that Ed had a spare twenty. He's not rich, just a clerk in a store here in town."

"We'll follow up on it this afternoon. Say, what day is this?"

Marci frowned a minute, then her brown eyes glittered. "Oh, I remember, it's Thursday, May 22. We've been on the job for four days now, or is it three?"

"Time enough we should have more done." Spur looked at her. "You have your fill of lunch so we can get back to work?"

Ten minutes later they talked to a young man in the hardware and tinshop. He looked to be in his twenties, short brown hair and an open, honest face.

"If you say that's the twenty I took to the bank for change, I guess it is. I didn't write down the serial number. You say it's a counterfeit?"

"Yes it is, Ed. Miss Philburton here is an expert from the Treasury Department and she can tell. What we need to know is where you got the bill?"

"Oh, that's easy. Only place I get a twenty is when I get paid, usual. This time it didn't come out of my pay envelope. I won it in a poker game at the Texas Belle Saloon over on First Street."

"Gambling, and you won the twenty," Marci said.

"Yes, matter of fact I won almost seventy dollars that night. I was thinking of turning into a professional gambler, but then I remember the times that I've lost half my wages. My wife would kill me."

"Are you sure you got the twenty from that saloon?" Spur asked.

"Oh, yes, no question. I bought fifteen dollars worth of chips to get into the game, then when I checked out I had over ninety dollars in chips that I cashed in. He gave me four twenties and some ones."

"You have any more of the twenties?"

"Sure, I think. Let's see. I paid my rent with one. He opened his wallet and took out three more twenties and handed them to Marci. "Usually I don't carry so much cash, but my wife doesn't know I won. I just kept it a little secret. Feels good to have sixty dollars in cash in my pocket."

Marci checked the bills, held one up to the light

and felt of it again. Then she looked at the serial numbers.

"One more of these is a counterfeit. I'll buy it from you for twenty good dollars. We're not supposed to do this, but in this case I hate to see you lose your winnings."

Ed had sweated and then grinned when he got back his sixty dollars in total again. "Oh, thanks. You don't know how much I appreciate this. I was wondering. How did the saloon get the phony currency?"

"That's what we're going to ask them," Spur said. They thanked Ed again and walked outside.

"How long has it been since you've been in a wild west saloon?" Spur asked the pretty lady beside him. Marci frowned.

"More than ten minutes, I can assure you. Let's go."

The Texas Belle Saloon was the best one in town, given as much to the gambling arts as to drinking. It had faro tables, poker tables, a wheel and several spots reserved for "21". Marci took a firm grip on Spur's arm as they went in the swinging doors of the establishment. It was sparsely populated this early in the afternoon.

Spur shot warning glances at a trio of cowboys at the bar and signalled for the barkeep to come down to talk.

"Are you the cashier for the gambling?" Spur asked.

"Right as rain, cowboy. Who are you?"

"I'm Spur McCoy. I work with the U.S. Government. We've picked up two counterfeit twenty-dollar bills that came from this saloon. I wonder if you'd mind telling us where you got them?"

"Bad bills? Not a chance. I check out every

twenty I see. I don't take no fifties or hundreds. Not that anybody ever has one to gamble with. No bad money from me."

Marci took a twenty from her pocket. "Is this an authentic U.S. Treasury Note?"

The barkeep/cashier/owner looked over the bill and nodded. "Good as gold."

Marci showed him another one. He approved that one. She showed him a third and he said it was fine too.

"Wrong on the last one," Marci said. "It's a counterfeit. The plate is perfect, but the ink and the paper are wrong. Compare the feel of the last two bills."

"Be damned. Pardon me, miss. I just never thought to check the feel of the paper. Don't think I could tell it again, but side by side I can tell the difference."

"Where did you get a batch of twenties lately?" Spur asked.

"Twenties, let's see."

"There was a poker game two nights ago. A man said he was a big winner and you paid him off in these twenties."

"Two nights ago. Not much happened last night. Two nights ago. Sparse crowd, only one poker table." His eyes lighted up and he grinned. "Yeah, I got it. One guy came in to play and gave me a hundred dollars worth of twenties. He had long hair like a mountain man and a full beard. Never seen him before. He gave me five twenties for a hundred in chips. In this town we don't get many chip buys like that."

"Mind checking your cash drawer and see if you have any twenties left? All five of those probably were counterfeit."

The barkeep looked at a drawer under the bar. He came back with three twenties. None of them had the right first four serial numbers and all were authentic.

"All good," Marci said. The barkeep let out a held in breath. "Damn, afraid I was going to lose another sixty dollars."

"Can you remember anything else about the man who gave you the hundred dollars? Did he talk rough or refined?"

"Come to think of it he was polite, well spoken. Sounded like one of them eastern college boys."

"About how old?"

"Hard to tell, slender, maybe five eleven now that I recollect him. I'd say under thirty. His eyes looked under thirty."

"Long, black hair?"

"Yeah. Now that I think, it was probably a wig."

They thanked the barkeep/owner of the place and went outside.

"Now you can say you've been in a wild west saloon where whores and drunks hang out," Spur said.

"Not one of my adventures I'll brag about. What now?"

"How many bad twenties have we recovered?"

"Nine."

"Keep checking the banks. That serial number is the payoff. There must be a lot more out there. Say he passed five at the saloon, then the stores. They must have figured to make a good test and be gone before anyone knew. We got ahead of them. I'll try another round of the printers."

"Tonight?" Marci asked.

Spur grinned. "Why not? We'll have a big supper somewhere good and then see if my bed is any better than that lumpy one you have in your room."

Marci laughed softly, touched his shoulder and went down the street toward the first bank.

The following morning, Clare Franks and Henry Rhonstadt boarded the 7:22 train bound for Austin. It was a three hour trip. They bought two tickets with a fake twenty-dollar bill and hurried on board. Each man carried a small leather folder that held $1,000 in bogus bills.

Each also had ten dollars in good money and another $40 in counterfeit.

"This is about the wildest day that I can ever remember," Clare said to Henry.

The other man stared out the window at the passing land. "I've got some second thoughts about our printer. We may have to dispose of him before we leave for good."

"Dispose?" Clare said. "I don't like the sound of that."

"He's getting out of line, trying to take over. He's just the printer. I have the plates. I *own* the plates."

Henry saw the long face Clare showed. "Come on, don't worry about him. This is the day we have some fun, like we used to talk about back there in Langtry at Judge Roy Bean's saloon."

Clare brightened. "Yeah, I'll try. Let's go over this again. How I'm going to deposit that money?"

"I've changed my mind. We'll both do it together. We're partners in a new restaurant we're starting in Austin. This is our development money from investors. Yes, I like the sound of that better."

In the bigger town, they went directly to the Texas First Bank of Austin and asked to see the manager. Both wore suits and ties and Henry had shaved closely that morning so his heavy beard didn't show through. He wore a proper hat which he now carried along with the leather case filled with $2,000.

The manager came to his desk where the two young men sat. Henry gave his spiel about just arrived in Austin to open a new high class restaurant. This bank had been recommended to hold their starting up fund in business capital.

"How much did you want to deposit?" the manager asked. He was about 50, pompous, acting as if he was wasting his time.

"We wanted to put a thousand dollars here and then a thousand in another bank. We'd heard about some bank failures here in Texas and we're not sure we should have all the money in one account."

The manager's frown vanished and he smiled. "Mr. Jones, I assure you that we can handle your two thousand dollar account nicely. Our bank is rock solid, basic real estate and only a few cash loans. I'd guess you'd want to have a book of bank drafts with your own account number on them for withdrawals for property purchase, rents, carpenters, that sort of thing."

"Yes, precisely, but we don't have our location yet, so you'll have to leave an address off the drafts."

"We have some blank ones that will be suitable. Now, there are some papers for you to sign. You said you're partners?"

A half hour later they were out of the bank. A clerk had counted the four stacks of bills and certified the amount—$2,000.

The manager shook their hands as they left and they walked sedately along for half a block before they exploded in exhilaration.

"We did it, little partner, we did it. We give them the special money and when we go back to draw out money, they give us the real thing. Because we ask for it in fifty dollar bills, there's no danger of getting back one of our own phony twenties!"

Clare waved his arms in the air. "Hot damn. I feel like celebrating. You mentioned something about a whorehouse in this town. Where are the girls?" For over two hours that afternoon they found the fun time girls.

Just before the bank's closing time at four o'clock, Henry went back inside and wrote out one of the bank drafts he had been given earlier. He wrote in the account number, 347, he had been given and made out the draft for $300. He took it to the teller.

"The manager opened our new business account this morning, and already I've found a piece of property for our new restaurant but I need to put three hundred dollars down on it today to get an option to buy it. Could I have it in fifties, please?"

The teller looked at the draft. "For that much, I'll have to get approval of the manager. I'll be right back."

The teller came back with the manager who was one big smile.

"Yes, Mr. Jones, that was quick work, I must say. You have found a property that you want?"

"We had a man here searching for us before we came. We do need the three hundred to secure the deal."

"Mr. Jones, no problem at all, you said fifties? That will be fine. We look forward to working with you on your new venture."

With the three hundred dollars in genuine green backs safely in his wallet, Henry Rhonstadt alias Jones, and Clare, caught the 5:45 train west bound and made it back to San Antonio just before nine o'clock that night after one short delay. They hurried to the back door of the print shop and slipped inside, then double locked the door and pounded on the special print room to get inside.

Osgood Jennings opened the door a crack, then swung it wide.

"Well, how did you do?"

Henry showed the three hundred in fifties and they all cheered. Henry sobered. "Fifty to you, Osgood, and fifty to our young friend for being such a good partner. I'll keep the rest for now. It will be a three way split later on with everything, so nobody worry. Right now we have certain expenses we need to handle with real money."

"What do you have for me to do?" Clare asked.

Osgood pointed to the work table. It was covered with twenty-dollar bills, stacks and stacks of them.

"All printed, our first three hundred bills, worth six-thousand dollars. All numbered with increasing numbers, except for the first four digits which is natural. All we need to do is trim off the edges and dirty them up and we're ready to start printing the next batch."

"No, I don't think so," Henry said. "Too dangerous to do it here. If some of those fake bills surface, here in our own back yard, we could have problems."

Osgood scowled. "You told me we'd work here for six months before we moved on. I won't leave my press. I worked too hard to get that fine a press to dump it."

"You can box it up and send it to wherever we land."

"Sure, and the detectives would know exactly where to look for us. There's no reason to leave here yet. We need to print as much paper as we can here before we go."

Henry seemed to go along with the idea. "It is tempting. But I don't like staying in one place any longer than we need to. The plates must have been missed by now. Where would the government detectives come first to look? To Langtry and then where? Where is the closest town with a printer? San Antonio." Henry paced the room.

Osgood bent to the task of trimming the bills one at a time on a hand levered paper cutter to be sure that the edges were trimmed correctly.

"I'm worried," Henry said. "Let's leave it this way. Until we hear about some federal agents in the area, we'll just sit fast."

Osgood grinned. "Good, good. Now we can get busy making more money. Clare, you need to make it all dirty after I make it clean and bright."

All that Friday, Spur and Marci had been trying to track down funny money. They had two reports from tellers, but when the bills were checked, they turned out to be regular currency.

"The tellers are getting suspicious of every twenty-dollar bill," Marci said Friday evening as they ate supper in the hotel dining room.

Spur had spent half the day checking the printers again. He asked for estimates on stationery this time. One printing plant looked suspicious but he had no way to test it. One of the five was closed due to a death in the family. "Can't fight the undertaker," Spur decided and called it a day.

Now he finished a cup of the new fangled ice cream in the hotel dining room and decided that he liked it. It was expensive and they only had one flavor today, strawberry, but it was good.

Spur eyed his helper and shook his head. "Damnit, Marci, I know I'm not doing enough. Either that or I'm trying to find the wrong man. I figured for sure I could track the robber, find him and he would lead us to the printer. It hasn't worked out that way.

"Right now it feels to me like I'm sitting around waiting for the counterfeiters to make a big mistake. Why haven't we found more of the bogus bills here in town? It's a tremendous temptation for them to spend the money in hand. At least a lot more than we've found. Why isn't this outfit doing that?"

"Maybe they're too smart to give themselves away," Marci said. "We need some more good sources who can identify the man who passed the bills. He wasn't a local man or someone would have recognized him."

"So what do we do next?" Spur asked.

Marci shrugged her shoulders and grinned. "Well, I know one thing we could do. It wouldn't help find the counterfeiters, but it sure would relax a detective who is so nervous and irritable that he's getting on my nerves."

Spur chuckled. "Sometimes I don't think you ever get enough. I can't remember you ever telling me, 'no.' Not in the past few days at least."

"That's a bad word when a girl is feeling the way I'm feeling. I've had a lot of 'yes's' all stored up and waiting. It's been at least a year since I've been so nice to any man as I have been to you. Done with your dinner food intake?"

"One more cup of coffee." He signalled to a waitress who brought the steaming pot and refilled both their cups.

"Tomorrow. We need to come up with some good strategy for tomorrow."

"Any other towns around close where they might have passed some of the money?" Marci asked.

"San Marcos, but that's forty-five miles up the tracks toward Austin."

"So why not Austin? They could pass a lot of cash there and be in and out on the train the same day. Didn't you say Austin was about ninety miles away?"

Spur nodded, he grinned. "Yeah, all right. Tomorrow we catch the early train and head up to Austin and check the banks there. It will take both of us most of the day. Must be ten banks in Austin by now. You want to get a good night's sleep tonight, or what?"

"What?" Marci asked.

Spur grunted. "Yeah, just about what I hoped you were going to say. I think my coffee cup is empty enough. Let's get up those steps and try to find your room."

"Wine," Marci said.

"What?"

"I want at least a bottle of wine for our party tonight. Where can we get some in town? The hotel has none, I tried once before."

"Wine and cheese and crackers. We'll make a regular feast of this. You head upstairs and I'll charge the possible stores in town. I thought I saw a place down the block that had food and some wines. I'll report back."

They both left. Spur was gone fifteen minutes and returned to Marci's room with a paper sack. He knocked on the door and she let him inside.

He pulled out a bottle of white wine, three kinds of cheese and three kinds of small crackers.

"Let the feast begin," Spur said.

Marci smiled at him and unbuttoned the top of her dress. "The wine feast comes next. I have something else for you for the first course. I sure hope you like them."

# Chapter Nine

By ten o'clock that Friday night, the bottle of wine was half gone. Some of the crackers and most of the squares of cheese that Spur had sliced with his belt knife had vanished as well. They lay on their stomachs on the bed, eating and sipping wine from the bottle where it sat on the straight backed chair they had pulled up to the bed.

"Three times so far?" Marci asked popping a square of cheese into Spur's mouth.

He chewed up the morsel, then nodded. "Three for me, but over twenty for you. I'll never understand women and the way you just can keep climaxing and climaxing and climaxing."

"It's a gift. We don't ask why, we just appreciate it." She lifted up and pushed back so she stood on her knees on the bed, naked and glowing. "Your turn to choose or mine?"

"My turn," Spur said, turning and bending so

he could slip one of her breasts into his mouth. He chewed for a minute, then bit her nipple until she winced.

"Wonderful pain, but don't do it too much or I'll be sore for a month."

"Is that what happened the last time you had a sex orgy?"

"This is not a sex orgy. We're merely making each other feel good and reducing tensions. It's good for our work."

Spur guffawed as he picked her up and dropped her a foot onto the lumpy mattress. "It's good for your crotch, that's what it's good for. Now admit it, you like to make love."

"Of course, silly. Why else would I be laying here stark naked with my legs apart and my knees lifted spreading myself open so you'd get the idea to poke yours into me?"

"I forgot the question."

She giggled. The wine had made them both a little giddy, but nothing interfered with their ability to perform.

"You choosing or not?"

"Yeah, on your hands and knees."

"That was the first time."

"So, it's going to be the fourth time and the seventh time and the tenth time."

Marci giggled. "With half a bottle of wine, you'll never make it past six."

"Bet?"

"Bet," Marci said. "If I lose you get to make love to me in this bed all night." She grinned. "I don't know why, but it sounds fair. You getting ready or do you want some more wine? I like the time when I got to pour it down your throat."

"Damned near strangled me."

"All part of a wild, fucking night in bed."

He lifted her and put her on her hands and knees. Then he began to gently slapping her round little bottom.

"Marci has been a bad girl."

"Yes, yes, more, more."

"No. I don't do that. It gets ugly and people get hurt. Having fun is more fun. Now hold still."

Four times Spur tried to mount her from behind, holding her firmly with his hands, then reaching around and grabbing both of her hanging breasts with his anxious fingers.

Four times it didn't work. He pushed Marci flat on the bed, rolled her over and set her up.

"Time for another little drink," Spur said.

Marci sat beside him toying with his limp whanger.

"I just never would have figured you for this. Three times and the great cockman, Spur McCoy, is not able to get it up anymore."

"Not me, it's the wine. What kind of wine did I get?"

He looked at the label, held it away from him and then read part of the fine print. "The only wine made in California that has 14 percent alcohol content. Whoa back there, Gert. Fourteen percent? That's stronger than some of the whiskey drinks I take."

"Fourteen percent what?" Marci asked.

She didn't wait for an answer, simply lifted the wine bottle to her lips and took a long pull on it. When she put it down she took in a deep breath and let it out with a whoosing sound.

"Not the least bit tipsy myself. I'm good for another ten go-a-rounds. What about you?"

"At least ten more."

They both sat down on the bed with the chair between them holding the wine bottle and the cheese and crackers. Spur tilted the bottle and drank, then tried a slice of cheese between two crackers.

"At least ten more times," Spur said. "You get to choose."

Marci sampled the white wine again, passed the bottle to Spur and grinned. "I choose an around the world festival. Once each way the whores make love around the world." She giggled, then her eyes slid shut and she fell over backwards on the bed.

Spur laughed. "Sounds like fun," he said to no one in particular. He set down the wine bottle and let himself fall backwards on the bed. He bounced once, then settled down. He looked over at Marci. Her eyes were still closed and her breathing came deep and even.

"Hey, party pooper. Come on, Marci, it isn't even late yet. Party time. Party time."

She didn't move. He tickled her under the chin and Marci giggled but never woke up.

"Oh damn, she's passed out." He looked at her again, then felt one eye close. "Hey, hey, not with some wine left in the bottle."

He tried to reach the bottle on the chair without sitting up. Impossible. He tried to sit up. It took him four attempts. Then he reached for the wine bottle. It moved just when he tried to pick it up and landed on the floor where it hit with a thump but didn't break. Wine flowed out of the neck of the bottle until it was precisely half empty.

Spur stared at the vacant place where the bottle used to be. He shook his head and flopped backwards on the bed again.

"Marci. Marci, your turn to choose," he said. Spur McCoy laughed out loud and a moment later he slept.

The next morning on the train heading for Austin, they sat beside each other facing forward. Spur rubbed his temples and growled. "Damn! Rubbing this way always helped before."

Marci winced at the sound of his voice. She sat with her head against the back of the seat resting gently on a cotton scarf she had brought for the trip.

"I'm never touching white wine again as long as I live," Marci said. "I hereby take the pledge. If I ask for some white wine again, you knock me down and sit on me."

Spur tried to grin but it wouldn't work. He massaged his temples. "You have any more of that powder the doctor in Washington D.C. gave you to take for headaches?"

"No, I used all of it. That was when you said you felt fine."

"I lied."

"I knew you did, but I took all the powder anyway. It should be working in a half hour."

"Working for you. Maybe I can get some sleep."

"White wine, never again."

The train wasn't crowded. The seat in front of them was empty. Spur pushed the back of the seat to its opposite position so he could put his feet up on the cushion and tried to scrunch down to get his head against the seat back.

"I'm too damn tall to do that."

After a slow recovery on the three-hour train ride, they arrived in Austin somewhat normal, and checked with the first store they sighted to find out the biggest banks in town. The storeman had a list, and they copied it down with names of the banks and locations.

Spur took half the names and Marci took the others, then they stopped and looked at each other.

"If yesterday was Friday, that makes today Saturday the 24th," Spur said. The banks are closed."

Marci looked as if she was ready to cry. She caught his arm and held on tight. "We could have been this miserable and stayed in the hotel. Now we'll have to come back on Monday."

Spur shook his head. "Maybe not. Let's find the chief of police or the sheriff, whoever is in charge here. He might be able to help us."

They found the County Sheriff's office and talked with the second in command. Both of them showed their federal identification and Spur told the deputy what they wanted. A half hour later, the elected sheriff came strolling in and they talked again.

"So, Sheriff, I need your help. This is a band of counterfeiters that could ruin Austin's economy. Say they passed ten-thousand dollars worth of bogus twenty-dollar bills in town. If we find them, by law we confiscate them offering nothing in return. Some small merchants could be wiped out."

"I see," Sheriff Vernon said. "How can we help you?"

A half hour later Spur and Marci had a list of the four biggest banks in Austin. The presidents of each bank or the managers had been ordered by the sheriff to come to their banks right away with the deputy sent to find them.

The first banker was upset by being pulled away from a family outing, but he assured Spur and Marci that his bank had not taken in a large cash deposit of $20 bills.

"I'd have been suspicious right away. Who would have all twenties when depositing a large amount of cash?"

The next two bankers claimed no large number of twenty-dollar bills had been taken in. Marci asked to check the teller's cash drawers and while finding dozens of twenty-dollar bills, none of them had the key four serial numbers and there were no counterfeits.

On the fourth bank they tried again. The manager frowned.

"Matter of fact, I did take in a two-thousand dollar deposit of twenty-dollar treasury notes yesterday. I thought it odd, but the two young men who deposited them were clean cut and said they were starting a new restaurant in town.

"Could we see those twenties, please?" Marci asked.

It took the president some time to open the safe and then to find the exact drawer where the twenties had been placed. Marci and Spur both caught up a bill and checked the serial number.

"A, two, eight, one, one," they said both in unison. "I'm sorry, sir, but these treasury notes are all counterfeit. I'm a Treasury Department expert from Washington D.C. and I can guarantee that these bills are fraudulent. We'll have to confiscate them with no compensation."

"They opened an account you say," Spur asked.

The bank manager sat down and used a white handkerchief to mop his suddenly sweating bow.

"Yes, yesterday. Then late in the day one of them came back and said he had found the property he wanted and wrote a draft on his account for three-hundred dollars. He wanted the money in fifty dollar bills."

"Smart, then he wouldn't get any of his counterfeit back," Marci said. "Was that the only draft?"

"Yes."

"Then you've only lost the three-hundred dollars. You should close out that account and if anyone wires for money from the account, I want you to go along with it, but don't send the money. Send to me at San Antonio the name of the individual and where and when the money is to be sent."

The bank manager sat down quickly.

"The three hundred. Is there any way that I can recover it?"

"Not that I know of. If we capture the men quickly enough they might have some of it left, but it would become evidence."

"So I'm out the three hundred. Damn!"

Marci packed the counterfeit money in a canvas bag she had brought along for that purpose and they thanked the manager and the sheriff and headed back to the train.

"Oh, Sheriff, you might check with the other banks Monday to see if any of them have any of these bills," Spur said. He took one of the bogus notes and tore it in half, giving the left half to the Sheriff. "If the first four serial numbers match the ones on this bill, it's almost certain that the notes are counterfeit. Send me a wire at the Drake Hotel in San Antonio if you find any."

The sheriff said he would and the two agents hurried to catch the afternoon train.

They sat side by side in the train seat and Spur grinned. "I feel a hell of a lot better now than I did this morning."

"And we have two-thousand dollars in funny money. I wonder how much they have printed?"

As the two agents rolled along the tracks toward San Antonio, the three counterfeiters huddled in the secret back room at the printing plant.

"Are you sure?" Osgood Jennings asked.

"Damn right I'm sure. The barkeep said he'd come damn close to losing a hundred dollars. He's the one I passed the hundred to when I wore the wig and moustache and played poker.

"He said two government agents are in town, at least one of them is from the Treasury Department. That means they're hunting for us. Somehow they found out about the bills we passed here."

"The bank would tell them," Clare said. "Bankers are trained to spot counterfeits."

"They sure didn't in Austin, did they?"

"So what are we going to do?" Osgood asked. "I knew we should have left town when we could."

"You want to print more money here," Henry said. "So the only thing to do is take care of this treasury agent. Somebody said his name was Spur McCoy. I just hope this isn't the same McCoy I've heard about."

"Take care of him?" Clare asked.

"Don't worry about it, kid. You won't get any blood on your hands. I'll take care of it all by myself, tonight."

"How?" Osgood asked.

"How? I'll find out his room number at the hotel. You said he's staying at the Drake. As soon as he goes to bed and gets asleep I'll slip inside and hit him with a blast from both barrels of a sawed off shotgun. Then I'm down the back stairs before anybody gets a door open."

"Won't work," Osgood said. "This Spur McCoy, I've heard of him, too. He's not Treasury, some kind of a government lawman. He'll expect something like that at the room. He won't be in it. Probably use another one and not tell the room clerk. I've got a better idea."

Henry scowled. "Yeah, what is it?"

"We put a letter in his hotel box telling him we have some information about the counterfeiters. If he wants it he should bring a hundred dollars in gold double eagles and come alone to some lonely spot. Then the three of us with rifles take care of him proper."

"Won't he smell us out?" Henry asked. "He'll be ready for something like that."

The printer shook his head. "I've seen this kind of thing done before. In on one of them. Worked like a greased pig through a chute. He'll think he's ready, but three to one, we got the odds and he can't win."

Henry grinned. "Jeeze, I knew I picked the right man here in town, Osgood. Let's write the damned note to Spur McCoy."

"I'm not much on writing," Osgood said.

"Hell, I'm the writer. Studied it enough. You have some paper and a pencil. We don't want nothing too fancy."

Fifteen minutes later, the three looked at the third draft of the letter that Henry Rhonstadt had finished.

"Spur McCoy, Drake Hotel, San Antonio, Texas. Mr. McCoy, I live here in San Antonio and I hear you're looking for some counterfeiters. I have some information about a printer I know that should lead you to the culprits.

"This information isn't free. You can't identify me or use my name. Bring $100 in gold double eagles to the back fence post on the back side of the livery pasture. Be there at one o'clock tomorrow, Sunday. I'll give you the information. It's well worth it. A Friend."

"Should do the trick," Henry said. "Now, how do we get it in his box at the hotel?"

Clare shrugged. "Easy. Just put it on the desk clerk's counter when he isn't looking and have the name on the envelope and the desk clerk will put it in the box."

Henry grinned. "Great idea, Clare. You're elected to get it on the counter without the desk clerk seeing you. Then make sure it gets in the federal cop's room box and we wait until tomorrow at noon."

Clare rubbed his jaw. Sweat popped out on his forehead and he slashed at it with his hand. He stood and turned around, hooked his thumbs in his belt and looked at Henry, then away.

"I can deliver the letter and all, but not sure I can shoot at a man. He never done me no harm. I ain't all that much in favor of killing people."

"Hell, Clare. He's just one man. Nothing important about him. He's in our way. Don't you want to get your twenty-thousand dollars? We figure we can pass sixty-thousand before they cover all the banks and everyone starts watching for these bills."

"Sure, I want the money. I need it to live in New York City for three or four years. But shooting a man in cold blood, I just don't know."

"Don't have to know, boy," the printer growled. "Easy to decide. You come with us and help us cut down that federal agent, or you don't get no money. None. That would make you a problem for us, now wouldn't it, boy? We might have to do some tall thinking about letting you go, even if you don't help us."

"Easy, Osgood. This is my little friend here. He'll come through, I know he will. I won't hear no more talk like that. Now, what do we have to do on these bills to get them ready to pass at another bank?"

They all went back to work on the paper money. Clare did his best to dirty up the bills and crumple them and make them look used. He left some of the bills in fairly good condition thinking that not all paper money looked trampled on.

"When you want me to take over the letter?" Clare asked.

Henry shrugged. "Right about now is as good a time as any. Wear a hat that comes down part way to shade your eyes, and don't look out of place. Drop the letter from under a newspaper. That's a good way. Put the paper down and hold the letter on the bottom of it. Then pick up the paper and the letter stays there."

Clare grinned. Now this part was fun. He took the letter sealed in an envelope with Spur McCoy's name on it and a folded newspaper, and walked over to the hotel.

The clerk was attentive at his station. Then three people came in to register. The eastbound evening train had just arrived. Clare went to the end of the counter and put down the paper. When the clerk looked away to help the new arrivals,

Clare lifted the paper, left the letter there and walked away.

He grinned as he told them about it back at the print shop. The other two laughed and clapped him on the back, then they went back to working on the money. Most of it was trimmed now and it sure looked real.

Clare had never seen so much money in his life. They had four-thousand dollars worth left in the room. Most of it was now stacked in piles of tens. He took a pile at a time and began working each bill in his "weathering" pan. It was the slowest job of them all.

Henry went over to where Clare was smoothing the bills.

"How's it going?" Henry asked.

"Uh . . . fine, I guess."

"You're worried about tomorrow, about that federal man?"

"Sure. I ain't never killed a man, never even tried. Don't sit good with me, Henry."

"Easy enough to fix. When time comes to do the shooting, you just aim so you miss the guy. I'll be close with my forty-four. I can take care of that jasper all by myself. Using Osgood as insurance, that's all. You do need to shoot though, so Osgood will hear it and so he won't want to strip you out of your cash. You see, that would mean more for him."

Clare looked up quickly. "I never thought of that."

"When you're dealing with an ex-convict like Osgood, you got to know all the ins and outs. Figure what he might do before he figures it himself. So tomorrow you just shoot around this McCoy agent. But be damn sure you don't hit me."

"Never do that, Henry. We planned our little caper with the Express car too long ago to let Osgood mess us up."

Henry nodded. "Yeah, you're right. Hey, we're pards here, little buddy, never forget that."

"Appreciate that, Henry. You're gonna be a character in one of my stories. I'm going to get started on a new story tonight, about this hapless kid who almost gets himself hanged because he hired on with a rustler thinking the guy was a real life rancher looking for more hands."

"Don't seem like that could happen."

"Sure as hell could. Did in fact, the day before I left to come over here. Kid damn near got hanged. He wasn't no more than sixteen-years old and from back east somewhere. He wanted to play cowboy and it almost got his neck stretched."

Henry grinned. "Sounds like a good story. Better'n I could think up." He lifted a handful of the bills that had been crumpled and let them fall back into the cardboard box where Clare had been dropping them.

"Damn, look at all this money. I never thought I'd see this much cash money in all my life."

"It ain't real, Henry."

"Looks damn real to me. Looked real to that banker. Wonder what he's gonna think when he finds out he has all them bad twenty-dollar bills?"

Clare grinned. "Damn, bet he pisses right in his pants.

Later that evening, Spur McCoy and Marci walked into the Drake Hotel feeling pleased with themselves. They had taken $2,000 in bogus bills out of circulation and got a precise description of two of the gang.

They checked their key boxes and Spur looked at an envelope the clerk handed him.

"Who left it?" Spur asked.

"Fact is I didn't see who did leave it. Any problem?"

Spur said there wasn't and tore open the envelope as they went up the stairs. He read the letter quickly and handed it to Marci.

"I think the counterfeiters just made that big mistake we've been hoping that they would."

# Chapter Ten

In Spur's room, Marci finished reading the letter and looked up, her pretty face clouded with a frown.

"You're not going."

"Of course I'm going."

"It's a trap. It's a set up to kill you."

"I've seen them before, Marci. I know how to handle them."

"How do you handle three or four men with rifles all aimed at your chest when you go to talk with this 'Friend'?"

Spur dropped on the bed and pulled off his boots. He wiggled his toes inside his socks and let out a satisfied sigh.

"There are three or four ways to deal with a set-up like this. The first is the safest, but produces the least bit of evidence—simply not show up. Not an option here.

"Another way is to get a trusty long range rifle, attach a telescope sight on it and zero it in to a quarter-of-an-inch at two-hundred yards. Then you find an advantageous location where you can see the meeting site. You get there an hour early and wait for the bad guys to show up."

"Be serious, McCoy. I don't want to get you killed over a lousy million dollars in bogus money."

"I feel the same way. The third and most used method of defusing something like this is to have six men hidden around the meeting site. We don't have six men.

"So I go to the next most used method. I go two hours early, scout the site, find the problems, locate myself a safe yet concealed hiding spot, then hunker down with a rifle and two six-guns and wait for the killers to show up."

"I'll be there, too," Marci said. "I can shoot."

"You won't be there if I have to tie you naked to the bed and gag you. I absolutely won't tolerate a pretty female getting into a shooting spree like this one. Besides, you might catch a bullet and I'd have to live with that for another sixty years."

He watched her. Marci scowled, started to say something and stopped. Then she turned around and walked to the window. She came back and began to say something again but stopped.

"I'd guess by now that we're straight on that. You really don't want to get out there where the hot lead is flying, do you?"

"No. Does that make me a coward?"

"Absolutely not. It makes you a wise woman. Besides, I'm not about to give these louts the satisfaction of gunning me down when about fifty men a hundred times as good as they are haven't been able to do the job."

She sat down beside him and kissed him, then pulled him down on the bed and kissed him again. When the kiss ended she snuggled against him and held on tight.

"Tonight I just want to lay here and go to sleep, with you holding me and me holding you. You know, sort of like we were married or something and didn't have to make love every night."

"Good idea. We both could do some catching up on sleep."

"Tomorrow is Sunday the twenty-fifth. I can't check the banks. I have no wish to go to church. There isn't even a big Sunday paper to read, so I'll probably just sleep in."

"Best idea you've had all night."

The next morning at six a.m., Spur left the bed gently so he wouldn't wake up Marci and dressed. The dining room was closed and the small cafe down the street hadn't opened yet. He hiked out to where he could see the house the suspect in the dynamite buying had rented between the big boarding homes. No smoke coming out the chimney. Why did this guy rent this house if he was never there?

Spur watched it until nine o'clock with negative results. He went back to the downtown section and found a cafe to his liking and had breakfast.

A rifle. He needed a long gun. At the Livery Barn, he talked to the owner and rented a rifle, a Spencer repeater, with seven rounds in the magazine tube through the stock, and one in the chamber. He took a box of 25 loose rounds and left a 20-dollar deposit. Spur was tempted to give the livery man one of the bogus treasury notes, but grinned instead and gave him a real twenty-dollar bill.

Spur left the livery walking. He saw the livery man eyeing him, but gave no indication of which way he would turn. Once he was shielded from the livery barn, he swung wide to the north until he could see the livery pasture. It ran for half-a-mile due north and had a three strand barbed wire fence around it. He was still two-and-a-half hours early for his one o'clock meet. That meant he should be there in plenty of time before the bad guys came to set up his ambush.

He walked out almost a mile, then headed back toward the far end of the pasture from the north. He saw the fence post that had been mentioned in the letter. The pasture ended in a point, with a massive post to hold the wire heading in both directions. The ground here was fairly flat, with one rolling mound toward the livery that almost blocked out the two story barn.

Spur checked the area carefully. About 50 yards from the fence post stood two small cottonwoods and some heavy brush. It could be the start of a small spring. He figured that would be the best spot for ambushers. They would be in the brush, maybe 20 feet apart.

He checked again, but there was no reasonable place to hide bushwhackers anywhere else within a hundred yards of the meeting site.

Now he tried to figure out where he would be. Again he found no good concealment. Some kind of scrub brush grew here and there, but not enough in any one spot to make a hiding shield. Most of it was too far away or too close.

Spur grinned. He saw places where tumble-weeds had piled up against some of the scrub growth. Yeah, why not move one of the bushes where he needed it. He picked the spot, then used his belt knife to cut off a dozen branches from a dozen different bushes. Most of the branches were three feet long. He carried them to a spot 50 yards this side of the meeting place and 100 yards from the cottonwoods.

Should work. He used his knife to dig holes in the hard ground where he could plant the brush limbs. He put half a dozen together and pounded down the ground around them until they stood up straight and looked like the other brush. Then he added a few to the sides and smashed two of last year's tumbleweeds against the front to make it look as if had been there all year.

He walked away from it to check. It looked as real as the others that dotted the area. Behind his shield, he scooped out the soil a foot deep to make a depression. The branches wouldn't stop a bullet. He found a few large rocks which he put immediately behind the bush. The foot high rocks and his depression in the dirt would be enough to give him some protection from rifle rounds.

He hadn't made up his mind yet just how to play it. He'd be in his position an hour before the others were set to arrive. From the location of the fence, he figured the bushwhackers would come from the other side of the fence, near the cottonwoods, so they would have no chance to see him as they arrived.

He'd play it as it fell and either charge the cottonwoods or shoot them up with the Spencer.

An hour-and-a-half before 1 p.m., Spur was ready. He placed the Spencer carbine with the barrel aimed at the cottonwoods, and lay out his six gun, then rested on his stomach behind his blind in a position so he could see through his viewing port between two of the big rocks.

Nothing moved ahead all the way to the Livery. It would be a long wait.

An hour before the meeting was set, Spur spotted two men with rifles walking up the outer fence line of the Livery pasture. They could have been townsmen going out pheasant hunting from appearances.

When they came up the fence 50 yards from the meeting spot, they stopped and talked. One pointed to the fence post, the other nodded and they walked a short distance over to the cottonwood and the head high brush. The two vanished into the brush.

Spur nodded grimly. It was to be a kill job. Somehow they never learned. But then most of them didn't have a second chance to bushwhack someone because they were dead.

Three times he saw the brush move below the cottonwood. Once he spotted an unblued tip of a rifle poke through the brush six inches off the ground where the sun glinted off it before someone withdrew it.

After that he saw no movement in the cottonwood patch. Spur remained rock still. At last he moved enough so he could get at his pocket watch. It was ten minutes until one o'clock.

Five minutes later, Spur saw a man riding a horse up the outside of the Livery pasture fence. He rounded the corner and rode directly to the large fence post and stopped. He looked around but evidently didn't see what he looked for. The man dismounted, walked the horse in a circle and mounted again.

Spur nodded. The man seemed nervous, so

Spur let him stew in his own sweat for a while.

Spur settled down to wait. Twice more the man dismounted and walked the horse in a circle. Once the circle came close to the cottonwood trees and he guessed that the man leading the horse had checked with his bushwhackers to be sure they were there. He came back to the fence post and sat on the mount waiting.

At a quarter after, Spur came from behind the brush and ran in a crouch until he put the horse and rider between himself and the bushwhackers in the cottonwoods. It would severely limit the fire by the bushwhackers.

Spur ran forward with the Spencer aimed at the man on the horse. The man saw him but made no move for a weapon.

"Spur McCoy?" the rider questioned when Spur came within 20 feet of him.

"Might be. Who the hell are you?"

"It doesn't matter. I understand you're a government agent interested in counterfeiting. I have some information you need. I can sell it to you for a hundred dollars in gold."

"I won't spend a hundred dollars without knowing that the information is correct and important."

"It is, I assure you. Would it help loosen your purse strings if I tell you I know who has been printing the twenty-dollar bills in town and passing them. I can give you his name and the place where he has his printing operation."

"That would be helpful, but how do I know that I'll stay alive long enough to use the information."

"What do you mean? I come with information, nothing else."

"Then why do you have two bushwhackers with rifles over there by the cottonwood trees?"

The man on the horse shook his head. "I'm sorry but I don't have the slightest idea what you're talking about. You saw me ride up here alone."

Spur squatted and sent a shot under the horse's belly into the brush around the cottonwood trees.

The man on the horse shrugged. "So you can shoot a tree. Do you want to buy the information, or not?"

"I'll have to think about it. Call off your two men in the trees, or someone will get hurt."

"I still don't know what you're talking about."

Even as he said it, the man on the horse had drawn his right handed revolver on the off side of the horse. Now he lifted it and got off a shot before Spur could jerk up the rifle and fire. He dove to the ground and heard the rifle snarl from the trees. The rifle round from the cottonwoods caught the rider in the shoulder and spun him half out of the saddle.

The next rifle shot drilled through the side of the rider's head, slamming him out of the saddle. He fell away from Spur, catching his foot in the stirrup, and the horse panicked and raced away, dragging the rider with him, the man's head slamming again and again into the hard dirt and rocks.

As soon as Spur saw the riflemen shooting at the rider, he sprinted ten yards to his tiny fortress and bellied down behind the rocks.

At once a rifle slug hit the foot thick rock in front of his head. Spur felt the boulder bounce back half an inch as it deflected the heavy rifle slug.

Two more rounds sliced through the dug-in bush branches, then there was a silence. Spur pushed the Spencer through the small hole between rocks and fired twice into the brush near the cottonwood tree. For a moment there was no response, then two more shots jolted into the boulders inside the bushy blind.

Spur moved enough to see through the hole and fired three times again, then paused. He heard a loud wail of pain and anger, then silence. That was followed by the loud voices of an argument. Spur jolted a new deadly messenger through the brush and the argument stopped.

A moment later two men ran from the cover of the brush toward the Livery. One turned and fired at Spur's position, then ran. Just as Spur was about to fire at the men, the second one stopped and turned and fired at him, making him jerk back behind the protection of the rocks.

When he looked out again, both men were vanishing over the small rise this side of the Livery that cut off his view. He turned to look into the countryside for the horse.

The runaway animal had stopped 200 yards away. Spur lifted up, dusted himself off and walked toward the mare. She stepped sideways as he came up slowly, facing her, talking softly. A moment later he caught the reins and put them over her head and she calmed.

The body lay crumpled and battered. Most of the back of the man's head had been smashed away but his face was hardly touched. Spur lifted the dead weight upward and kicked the corpse's foot out of the stirrup, then hoisted him over the saddle face down. The body sagged there, held in place by its own weight as Spur started back towards town leading the mount and its grisly burden.

Ten minutes later he stopped in front of the courthouse and asked about the sheriff. A deputy came running out and checked the corpse. He said that Spur should wait, the sheriff would be right out. A man marched out of the courthouse and looked at Spur a moment, then walked up directly to him.

"Sir, if you're the sheriff of this county, I'd like to turn over a body to you. My name is Spur McCoy and I'm with the United States Secret Service."

The man who stopped in front of Spur was in his early forties, chunky with soft blond hair and no uniform or gunbelt.

"I'm Sheriff Townsend. Looks like this one is dead sure enough. You better come inside and fill out a report on this. How'd he die anyway? Looks like he got dragged by his horse a considerable way."

Inside the small sheriff's office, Spur filled out a report on the death of the man at the hand of a gunman unknown. The bullet hole was still evident in the man's head.

"You know who he is, Sheriff?"

"Can't say that I do. We'll prop him up on a door outside the general store. Somebody will recognize him and tell us. You for sure work for the government?"

"That I do, Sheriff. I'm here with a treasury agent to find some counterfeiters. This was one of them, I'd imagine. He fits the description. Oh, mind if I check his pockets?"

Sheriff Townsend didn't and Spur found ten of the bogus twenty-dollar bills. He confiscated them and put that in his report, then went to find Marci. She stood outside the courthouse looking at the corpse.

"Bet that's one of the counterfeiters," Marci said. "Fits that last description we have. Did you kill him?"

He took her arm and pulled her away from the gruesome sight and walked her down the street. Over a dish of strawberry ice cream, he told her what happened.

"So if he's one of the counterfeiters, where are the rest of them? What about those two who got away?"

"They're the ones we need to find. Best place to look is at all of the printing shops. If there was a circuit court judge in town we could get a search warrant. I guess we'll have to be invited in to look around.

"That's our next job. We start with the first printer we find and look into every nook and closet in the place."

"Oh, I had an idea," Marci said. "Maybe I can save us some time. Once in Chicago we worked a case where we broke it by checking the burn barrels in back of printers. One day we found some edges of paper that had been poorly printed money. We caught the guy that same afternoon."

"Let's give it a try."

They worked three printers' back doors and alleys and in all three of them they found certificates and bad printing and burned edges of wedding invitations and death notices, but none of partly burned twenty-dollar bills.

On the fourth one the fire had not quite gone out. Spur fished around in the barrel with a stick and stabbed a piece of paper and pulled it out. It was only singed around the edges but had an almost perfect green ink print job of the back of a twenty-dollar Treasury Note.

"Jackpot!" Spur said. "We've got him. Warrant or no warrant, we're going in this place. We can get around the no warrant problem somehow. Last time I was here the printer gave me a quote on some stationery. I'll give him the job this time."

Around front they knocked on the locked door. No one answered.

"It's Sunday," Marci said. "He must not be open on Sunday. Nobody else is."

"Then I'll try the lock."

He looked at it a moment. It was one of the old-fashioned skeleton key locks. A piece of wire and he'd have it done. He took a folded wire from his pocket that he carried for emergencies, twisted the end of it to resemble a skeleton key and tried it. It didn't work. He tried again. Marci giggled.

Spur put the wire in his pocket and stepped back from the door. Suddenly he lunged forward and kicked hard with the sole and heel of his big boot directly beside the door handle. The jolt broke one foot square pane of glass in the door and bounced the whole door open.

Spur motioned for her to be quiet and stepped through the open door. His .45 Colt came into his hand and he moved without a sound around the counter and into the back room. Marci went right behind him.

He saw that the place was deserted, but there was that locked section to the left that he never had seen into. One time the printer said the man who owned the building had some display cases and other retail equipment in the room.

Spur and Marci worked over to the door and Spur saw that the outside padlock was off the door. He gently tried to turn the knob. It turned but the door didn't open.

Spur put his ear flat against the door and listened. A few moments later he came away and nodded.

"Two men talking inside. Doing something else but I'm not sure what. I think they have the door barred from the inside. Not a chance we can bluff our way in or break in, so we settle down and wait."

They found some filled boxes ten feet away and sat on them, leaning against the wall.

"How long will it be," Marci asked.

"Who knows? Ten minutes, ten hours. We don't have anything better to do. They must do the money printing inside at night or Sundays and keep up appearances with a legitimate print shop out here. I can't remember this gent's name, but he was always short and gruff when I talked to him. Gave me the idea that he didn't trust anybody farther than he could throw his press."

Just then they heard a bolt pulled back and the door edged open an inch. Spur had his Colt in his hand and stood without a sound. He motioned for Marci to stay where she was. He saw her fumbling in her reticule for her .38 and he prayed she didn't try to use it.

Spur moved up on the wall side of the opening door and waited, his Colt aimed head high where the door would open.

# Chapter Eleven

The door banged open from a hard kick from the inside and at once a shotgun blasted past Spur and into the print shop. Buckshot lanced through the door shredding some boxes of paper 20 feet away. Spur was safe behind the wall. Marci had remained where they had waited and was out of the line of fire.

"Might as well drop the scatter gun and walk out with your hands in the air. You're trapped in there and you know it."

There was no answer.

Spur could hear some whispering from inside but not the words.

"Hold it out there, we're coming. We won't give you no trouble. No sense getting killed over cash we'll never spend."

"Now you're making sense," Spur said.

More whispering from inside.

"No! I won't do it. I'm getting out of here." The voice came high and angry from inside the secret room. Then Spur heard running footsteps and a blast from a six-gun followed by a scream and something hitting the wall hard.

"Oh, God but that hurts. Why did you shoot me, Osgood?"

A minute later Spur heard more sounds near the door. Then the first voice he had heard came from close by.

"McCoy, that must be you. I'm coming out, but I'm the one in charge, not you. I've got a kid in here as a hostage. My .45 will be in his mouth. We're tied together so you don't have any choices.

"I'm walking out of here with a satchel and the kid. You so much as blink cross-eyed at me and the kid loses the top of his head and you'll be next. You understand what I'm saying?"

"Right. Who's the hostage?"

"Never mind. Your job is to keep him alive, and that means letting us walk out of here and out the back door. If you poke your head out there within ten minutes I'll see you, and the kid gets himself suddenly dead. You understand me?"

"Yes, Osgood, I think I do. You were the printer. You must be good. You'll never live to spend that cash, you know that, don't you?"

"Shut up. No more talk. We're coming out now. The kid got himself shot in the shoulder so he's bleeding some, but he ain't near dead. Now stand back, lay flat down on your belly on the floor. You move, the kid gets it."

Spur backed up and went on his stomach.

Two men shuffled out of the side room. They were tied together and the older man had the muzzle of his revolver in the young man's mouth. The kid's eyes were wild with fear.

"Stay down government man, don't try nothing. No sense the kid dying just yet."

He moved toward the back door in shuffling steps. They were bound together face to back which made walking easier. Osgood didn't see Marci crouched by the far wall. Spur prayed that she didn't try to shoot.

Another step, and another one. It seemed to Spur that getting the 30 feet to the alley door would take a year. At last he heard the back door open.

"Stay down, government man, and the kid lives."

Then the two were out the alley door. Spur grabbed Marci and they ran for the front door.

"He said stay down," Marci cried.

"He'll never know. We get out the front door, you go down to the end of the block the far way, turn down the side street and look down the alley. He has to go one way or the other. He'll probably go the near way, so I'll be there. Just depends if he still has the boy with him what I do. But I figure the boy won't be with him. You understand what to do?"

"If he comes my way?"

"Watch where he goes. Stay out of sight. Keep your weapon out of sight or he'll kill the kid for sure. Now go."

Spur watched her run along the boardwalk, her skirts flying. He rushed the other way. A few moments later he peered around the corner of a building next to the alley. At first he saw nothing. Then a minute later he saw Osgood. It was the same man with the dark blue work pants and lighter blue shirt. He had the same leather traveling bag evidently loaded with counterfeits. Only now he sat astride a big black horse that looked strong.

Osgood rode toward Spur. The agent waited at the alley, his six-gun ready. It would be an easy shot.

Before Spur could stop him, a big man in a farm wagon drove into the alley and stopped there, looking around. His wagon and team of four took up a lot of room on this side of the alley.

"Hey there. You at the street," the man in the wagon called to Spur. "You know if the hardware store is up this alley, or is it the next one? I got to pick up some of that barbed wire."

As the farmer talked, Osgood must have sensed the danger. He ducked off the side of his mount and galloped past the team of four and the high farm wagon. Spur didn't have a shot. Osgood turned up the side street and was gone.

Spur swore at the farmer, looked up the street for a horse. Two men rode toward him, cowboys from the way they were dressed. He ran toward them waving two twenty-dollar bills.

"Need to rent your horse," Spur bellowed. "I'm a federal lawman. Got to chase a counterfeiter. Which one of you wants to earn forty dollars?"

The closest one jumped off his horse and gave Spur the reins. He grabbed the money and turned back toward town. "I can gamble and whore all the rest of the day on this," he said.

Spur mounted, kicked the working cow pony in the flanks and she responded, jolting forward. He was in time to see the big black galloping up the street and turn to the left away from the main part of the town.

Spur turned down the next street to the left and caught sight of the black again, moving north on this new street, out of town. He was three blocks behind the counterfeiter, but the little cow pony was gaining on the black. They couldn't gallop much farther.

That's why they call them quarter horses, Spur decided. They could flat out gallop for only a-quarter-of-a-mile. A real race horse could go flat out for a-mile-and-a-quarter if it had to.

He pushed the cow pony for another two blocks, then let up on her to an easy lope. The black ahead had turned down another street that wound up in the edge of the Texas prairie.

Now there was nowhere to hide. Only one more house out this far: a neat little place painted white with a white picket fence, a small barn and a big garden. To Spur's surprise, Osgood slanted toward the place and rushed inside without knocking.

Spur was still 200 yards behind the counterfeiter. Now the man had a fort. Spur stopped when he was 100 yards away and looked over the house. He wasn't about to ride up to the front door. There probably was a rifle in the house, but had Osgood found it yet?

Spur rode around to look at the side of the house. Only one window and it was high up on the second floor. Hard to see out of. He kicked the cow pony in the flanks and raced up to the blind side of the house. He ground tied the mount and edged around to the corner of the house where he could see the front door. Osgood stood there with his six-gun pressed against a young woman's throat. He looked both ways.

"McCoy, you're around close somewhere. Got

me a new hostage, one who can go with me longer. This one ain't bleeding to death. You so much as show your face around the corner of the house and I kill this one and use her body as a shield as I come and kill you. Understand?

"We're going to the barn and get another horse. Then we ride, and you ride the other way or she dies. A shame a pretty little thing like this to get all shot up, ain't it? Now stand back or she's dead."

Spur swore softly and watched as the girl caught the black's reins and she and Osgood walked to the barn with his revolver's muzzle hard against her chest. Five minutes later a door opened and the girl rode out on a bay, with Osgood right behind her. No time to do anything.

Spur knew that Osgood wouldn't kill his hostage, not unless he had a good shot at Spur as well. She was his ticket to freedom, or so he thought.

Spur held back as they turned and rode back toward town. They were a little west of town now, and Spur wondered where Osgood was going. He still carried his satchel that must have thousands of dollars worth of counterfeit bills in it.

The Secret Service Agent saw Osgood look back and see that Spur followed. The man yelled something Spur couldn't make out, then he fired his six-gun seemingly at the girl. But she didn't move or cry out. A bluff. Spur moved closer now until he was within a hundred yards of them.

Spur heard the trouble before he saw it. The long wailing whistle of the train. It was the two-fifteen heading west. Osgood must be aiming for the tracks hoping to stop the train and board. Spur rode flat out on the cow pony for a hundred yards until he was only 30 yards away before Osgood heard him coming. Spur fired five shots at the counterfeiter. He was too far away for any accuracy and on the pair of bouncing horses the shooter and the target were both in a constant state of motion.

Spur reloaded his six-gun as he rode. The tracks came up out of a depression and were much closer than Spur thought they would be. He could see the smoke from the train just pulling out of San Antonio a half mile away. It would be here in only a few minutes.

Ahead, Osgood rode onto the tracks. He dismounted and made the girl get down. He positioned her in front, then himself and the two horses behind him. The engineer would see him in plenty of time to stop. To help him decide to stop, Osgood held up his six-gun so the sun would glint off it.

Spur got within 30 yards again. He couldn't risk a shot. Osgood had pulled the woman close to him, with one arm around her waist pinning her back against his chest.

"You've lost, McCoy. Give it up. You know you ain't gonna shoot long as I got this pretty here. So go away."

Down the tracks, Spur sensed when the engineer saw the obstruction on the rails and eased off on the throttle. At 400 yards he began applying the brakes and the train rolled to an easy stop ten yards from Osgood. The printer ran up to the engine and held the engineer under his gun as the girl scrambled off the tracks. The train edged forward and the horses snorted and walked down the side of the grade to the sparse grass beyond.

Spur couldn't hear what Osgood told the engineer, but a minute later the counterfeiter stepped into the cab and the train began to roll forward. Spur had ridden toward the back end of the ten-car train as Osgood talked. Now he broke for the tracks, spurred his mount up the side of the grade and caught the train before it had speeded up to ten miles an hour. Spur swung onto the side of the caboose and climbed to the top of the car.

He'd heard about running along the tops of a train but had never needed to do it. The distance between cars never seemed to be much when he was going from one to the next from down below.

Now the seven feet seemed longer. He held his breath and jumped, landed safely on the first passenger car and ran down the top of the swaying train.

He made it to the third car from the engine when Osgood lifted up from the wood car right behind the engine and pumped three rounds down the top of the cars. They missed Spur but made him change his tactics. He swung down at the next car connection and stepped into the passenger compartment.

Casually, Spur walked through the car and through the next one, then soon came to where the last passenger car was connected to the wood car that supplied fuel for the big Baldwin engine's boiler. The entry door was locked from the outside.

Spur went back to the far end of the first car and climbed back to the roof. He held his six-gun in front of him and moved forward with as little noise as possible. The rattle of the train cars and the click-click-click of the wheels on the rail joints drowned out what sounds he made.

A head edged up from the front of the wood car and Spur slammed a lead round into the metal of the car just in front of the head which jolted downward at once. Spur ran forward a dozen feet, then stopped and dropped to his knees.

Osgood lifted up and fired twice without aiming down the top of the car. By the time he saw Spur flat on his belly, he started to drop back down, but Spur's first shot nailed him in the shoulder and he jolted backwards with a cry of pain.

Spur raced the last 20 feet of the car and saw Osgood at the back of the Baldwin 4-4-0 furiously pounding on the connecting box between the wood car and the engine. Spur shot into the air, but Osgood kept hammering with a chunk of wood better suited to the engine's steam boiler.

Spur lifted his six gun again aiming at Osgood, but before he could fire, there was a lurch that threw him off balance. He nearly fell as the passenger car he rode on suddenly slowed and the engine pulled away from the wood car and the rest of the train. Spur fired one more time, then ran down the stacks of wood on the wood car and leaped at the back of the engine. Osgood stood there laughing at him.

But the run and the leap carried Spur over the eight feet between the back of the wood car and the small platform on the Baldiwn engine. Spur grabbed on, hoisted himself up and by then Osgood came to life. He swung with his right arm, but his left hung useless at his side.

Spur slammed his fist into the man's mid-section and clubbed his heavy Colt down across Osgood's head.

Osgood clutched the satchel against his chest as his eyes flickered. Before Spur could grab him, he fell off the short platform in back of the boiler and hit the tracks, rolling twice.

The engineer had cut power on the engine as soon as he saw the connector come loose. They were on a slight downgrade and the wood car and the passenger cars rumbled along twenty feet behind the engine now.

Even before Spur could shout, Osgood looked up from where he lay on the tracks and stared at the engine, then the wood car's heavy steel wheels smashed into him, crushing him and cutting his torso in half, obliterating the start of a scream. The treasured traveling bag tumbled down the grade as the train swept past.

It took the engineer a-quarter-of-a-mile to re-connect the train to the engine and get it all stopped. Spur jogged back along the tracks to the grisly remains. He pulled Osgood's legs off the tracks and put them beside the rest of his battered body that had been slammed down the right of way by the 20 heavy railroad car wheels which had hit it.

A dozen yards away he found the bag that Osgood had been protecting. Spur opened it and looked at a fortune in twenty-dollar bills. A fortune if they had been real. He checked the first four digits of the serial numbers. Yes, all were A-2811. The bills weren't worth the paper they had been printed on.

Spur looked down the tracks. He could barely see smoke coming from San Antonio. Must be five miles to where they boarded the train. The Secret Service Agent shrugged and strode out, first taking steps too short on the ties, then trying to miss every other one.

He whiled away some of the time by walking on the shining rail. He used to do that as a boy. Now it came back and he swung along with the thousands and thousands of dollars worth of worthless counterfeit money as his balance bar.

Long before he found the horses, he had opted to go down the grade to the edge of the prairie and walk there where he had only to dodge an occasional rock and prairie dog hole.

As he expected, two horses remained nearby. The third horse the girl had been riding was no longer there. He mounted the cowboy's cutting horse and picked up the reins of the black and rode back to town.

He had another session with the sheriff.

A half hour later, Spur had written his report for Sheriff Townsend. He told two sheriff deputies with a wagon where they should go to find the remains, then displayed the counterfeit money in the satchel to the sheriff.

"Damn, all that dumped in town would have caused us a lot of trouble." the sheriff said.

"A great deal of trouble. Now, the only other trouble I have is to be sure I find those printing plates before anyone else does. He scowled. The plates were worth more than the bills that Osgood tried to get away with. He rummaged in the bag of bills. No, the plates were not there. A shiver stabbed down his spine and he ran outside.

Spur caught the deputies who were going after Osgood's body.

"I'll lead you out there and save you some time,"

Spur told them. "First we need to make a stop by the printer's place and be sure it's locked up. Don't want anyone stealing from him."

At the print shop, Spur hurried inside and checked the press inside the secret room. The engraved plates of the $20 Treasury Notes, front and back, had been taken out of the press. Yes, Osgood would have them with him. They could even have been smashed or cut in half by the train wheels.

Or somebody could have happened along, found the body and stripped it of the plates, and Spur's search would begin all over again. Damn!

Outside, he mounted up and gave the wagon men general directions: Hit the tracks out of town and follow them on the north side until they found the body. Spur left them with gaping mouths as he turned his mount and whipped it into a gallop through town and out west along the tracks.

He had to be in time. He had to be the first one to find the body. Unless some preacher found him, or a priest giving him last rites, and they found the plates and turned them in as an honorable citizen would. Sure, even a priest.

The horse slowed and Spur brought her down to a sedate walk. The place couldn't have been more than five miles outside of town. It was along a desolate stretch of the tracks not near any buildings, ranches or streams. With luck the plates would still be on the dead body.

Spur recognized a small cottonwood, and then another, and at last he saw the spot where he figured the train had stopped. Another few minutes.

No one lurked along the tracks.

Then he could see the body ahead. A solitary hook nosed hawk circled high overhead, evidently trying to decide if the dinner waiting below was dead or not. Birds were patient creatures.

Spur McCoy was not. He slid the horse to a stop and leaped off, scrambled up to the body and pulled open Osgood's jacket. He had put on a light weight jacket before he left the print shop. Why? To hold the plates in the pockets?

Nothing at the inside top pocket. He bent and flipped back the side of the jacket. It hit with a thump on the dead hip. Maybe! He felt the pocket from the outside. Yes, something hard. He pushed his hand inside the pocket and came out with something wrapped in paper and tied shut with a string. Spur used the point of his knife and cut out a section of the paper on one corner.

"Yes!" he said out loud. It was one of the missing plates. He pulled the other flap of bloodied coat out from under the stiffening body. The second plate rested securely in Osgood Jennings' second pocket. Both looked undamaged, perfect.

Spur sat on the sand and dirt and laughed. He would have been ridden out of the Secret Service if he'd passed up the engraving plates that could sink the nation's economy and someone else had found them.

Lucky old him.

Spur sat there for five minutes staring at the wide open eyes of Osgood. What had made him go over the side and shoot the hostage and then kidnap the girl? He probably would never know.

Spur stood, felt in his shirt pocket to be sure the two plates were there, then stepped on board his borrowed horse and let her walk the six miles back to town.

He met the improvised meat wagon halfway to town and told them to just keep moving. He had to inspect the body before they got there, but he was done and the corpse was all theirs.

Back in town, he rode the main street for ten minutes, back and forth, until a cowboy yelled at him from the boardwalk.

"Hey, you looking for me?"

Spur waved at him. "You the hombre who rented his horse to me?"

"Deed I am."

"How much did I pay you?"

"Forty sinful dollars. Problem is, I don't have a penny of it left."

"Sounds about right." Spur stepped down from the horse and handed the young man the reins. "That's a good animal. Served me well. Give her a good feeding of oats when you get her back to the ranch."

Spur turned and hit the boardwalk ready for some food. He'd missed dinner again. No wonder he never got fat. He walked half a block and was ready to go into a cafe when a voice stabbed out behind him.

"Spur McCoy, don't you move another step!"

# Chapter Twelve

Spur grinned as he turned around. No need to go for his Colt in home leather. He knew the voice. She stood four feet away, a frown on her face but her hands nervous at her sides wanting to reach out and touch him.

"You could have at least told me that you were not dead somewhere."

"Sorry, I got rather busy."

"So I've heard. Cut in half?"

"I'm afraid so. Those rail car wheels are unforgiving." He took out the two engraving plates and showed them to her. "I figure since you're the agent in charge from Treasury you should take possession of these two chunks of metal."

Her eyes widened and she looked up at him a grin stabbing through her frown until her face was wreathed in a wonderful smile.

"Both of them? You really got them?"

He told her how he overlooked them the first time. "Not clear thinking, Marci. I knew those plates were worth more than one bag full of currency. It just figured that Osgood would have them with him. He must have been planning on getting away before we came."

"He was," she said. "Oh, I found the boy in the alley where Osgood dumped him. Wrapped up his shoulder and got him to a doctor who patched him up. He'll live. He also talked his head off." She slowed and stared at him. "You look hungry."

"How could you tell?"

"You're drooling and watching that cafe door like a wolfhound scenting his nightly bone."

"Lead on and I'll follow. Tonight I'm hungry enough to eat that wolfhound, bone, tail, hair and all."

Inside they found a table, ordered and then Spur looked at her.

"So, what did the boy say about this operation?"

"Everything. He's from up near Langtry where the goods were stolen. A rancher's son up there. Wants to be a writer, if you can imagine that."

"He was in on the robbery?"

"No. He was too well-known up there. The first dead man, Henry Rhonstadt was the brains behind it all. He and Clare, that's the kid's name, used to drink up at Judge Roy Bean's saloon at Langtry. They cooked up the idea of robbing a railway express car, hoping to get lucky and catch some cash sent through the registered mail, or there would be some cash or gold in the safe."

"But this Clare didn't do the robbery?"

"Right. Henry hired a man for fifty dollars and

booted him on his way to California without telling him how good the robbery had been as soon as it was over. No chance to find that Jasper."

"Henry bought the dynamite?"

"Yes. He knew the printer from before. Osgood had spent time in state prison for manslaughter. Killed two whores down in Houston. Henry figured Osgood would be safe and not go running to the authorities."

"So when Henry got shot yesterday, it wasn't an accident."

"True. Osgood bragged to Clare that now they had one fewer partner to split with."

Their food came and both ate with gusto, she finishing her steak before he did but hers was normal-sized, his was a two-pounder with all the side dishes.

A half hour later, they got back to the business at hand.

"So when did this Clare come on the scene?"

"He had to work on his father's ranch during a roundup, but he got here Thursday. Is this Sunday or Monday? Anyway, he came and said they put him to work making the money look used, rubbing it with dirt and crumpling them up and straightening them out."

"Then he was the other man who made the deposit up at Austin?"

"Right."

"So he's in jail now charged with counterfeiting?"

She looked away. "No. I don't think we should charge him. The fact is, I made a promise to him that if he testified against Osgood, we'd get him off free and clear. He's only twenty-one. This is the first time he's ever been off the ranch. He was just mad at his father and mixed up."

"Why did he get shot in the print shop?"

"Oh, yes, I didn't tell you. Osgood said they were ready to go. They had heard us break down the front door. Osgood gave Clare the shotgun and told him to kick the door open and blast anyone he saw with the scattergun.

"Clare said he'd been afraid of Osgood ever since he bragged about what a good shot he had made to kill Henry. Clare said he refused to use the shotgun. He ran for the door and Osgood shot him with his six-gun. Then he used him as a hostage and a shield, dumping him in the alley as soon as he got to the horse he had tied there.

"Clare said that's when he figured the printer was going to kill him. Osgood had brought only one horse figuring he'd leave alone one way or the other."

Spur pushed back his dish that had held strawberry ice cream and rubbed his face with his right hand. "Where is Clare now?"

"He's in my room at the hotel waiting for us to come up there."

"You say he agreed to testify against Osgood long before you found out the printer had died?"

"Yes. While the doctor fixed up his shoulder we worked it out. The sawbones can testify to that. Clare said he was a stupid kid and hadn't really thought through what he was doing. Actually, all we can charge him with is being an accessory to converting some counterfeit to his own bank account. He never tried to profit by it. He never drew out any of the money."

"His partner did."

"But Clare didn't." She pushed closer to Spur. "I guess I believe the kid and like him. He doesn't belong in a prison. His father is partly to blame."

She told Spur about the pretend hanging his father set up for the surprised rustlers.

"That man needs some help," Spur said. "Doing that to his own son."

Spur pushed back and pulled her chair out for Marci. They paid for the meal, then walked toward the Drake Hotel.

"Does he know that Osgood is dead yet?"

"Not if he has stayed in the hotel room the way I told him to."

"Let's go have a talk with the boy. Looks like the main players are both dead. No sense in dragging the boy into it any deeper than he is. If I like the sound of the kid, I might go along with you. Otherwise, I'll file the charges myself if you don't want to."

"Give him a chance. I think you'll like him. Oh, his whole name is Clarence Franks."

Spur stopped in the middle of the boardwalk. "Was his father a colonel in the cavalry?"

Marci grinned. "Yes, how in the world did you know that?"

"His name is Colonel Duncan Franks. Knew him on a campaign against the Chirachaua out in Arizona. He was a by the book soldier and too bad for anybody who didn't do it that way. Never did like the guy, but he got the work done. The generals loved him and his men hated him. He used them like pawns in a chess game, figuring how many men he could afford to lose on each phase of an operation. I was along on an official inquiry at the time, undercover investigating another man in the command.

"A year or so after that, his unit got shot up bad

in an attack that went wrong and they gave him a medical discharge. Yes, be interesting to see what kind of whelp comes from Colonel Franks."

Marci's frown deepened. She waggled a finger at Spur. "Now listen here, McCoy. I don't want you visiting the sins of the father on the son. I don't want you punishing the kid just because you didn't like the colonel."

"I wouldn't do that. Let's go see the boy."

"Let's go past the telegraph office. I want to wire the good news to my boss in Washington."

Spur growled. "You do that and my boss will know it within an hour or two and I'll get a new assignment before noon tomorrow. I figured we could stall a day or two and then send the wires."

"What could we do for a day or two?"

"We haven't even inspected the site of the robbery. At the same time we can meet Judge Roy Bean, the only law West of the Pecos, and see his famous saloon and court room."

"That's out in Langtry, right?" she asked.

"Fact it is. If the boy is going back that way we could even stop by and see his pa."

"You old softie."

"Not true. What's right is right. I still haven't made up my mind about Clarence yet. Depends on one thing I need to ask him."

"What?"

"Need to ask him. Let's go up to your room."

A short time later they knocked on the door and went into Marci's hotel room. Clare Franks sat on the chair near the window looking out. His left shoulder and half his arm were bandaged and his arm strapped tightly to his chest.

"We meet again, Clare," Spur said. "I hear

you're ready to testify against Osgood."

Clare stood and nodded. "Yes, sir. I've told Miss Philburton that. I never really had much to do with the operation except rubbing some of those bills in dirt."

"Yesterday in back of the livery pasture, did you shoot at me?"

"Oh, no sir. Henry told me I should fire, but I didn't have to aim anywhere near you. Just so Osgood knew I was firing. He couldn't tell where I shot."

"Osgood is the one who killed Henry?"

Tears welled up and spilled over Clare's eyes. He rubbed them away and nodded. "Yes. Osgood said he planned it that way. He wanted to kill Henry first, and then you. He was mad as hell that he didn't get you, too, but you came up behind the horse and he didn't have a shot."

"I knew where you were, Clare, so I planned to keep you both shielded by the horse and Henry."

"It sure worked."

"When did Osgood decide to leave?"

"Right after we got back from the pasture yesterday afternoon. Said you'd find him eventually. He had planned on riding out aways and flagging down the train and getting on board so nobody in town would know he was gone."

"He say anything about taking you with him?"

"Yeah, he said we'd both go, but I had a feeling he wasn't going to. I wanted to stay at the hotel last night, but he said it was a waste of money. He had blankets and two old cots there we used most of the time."

"Surprised when you woke up alive this morning?" Spur asked.

Clare looked up in amazement. "Yeah, how did you know? Then I figured he must have decided he needed me to help him get out of town. Which it turned out, he did."

"I heard an argument in the print room. Was that about using the shotgun?" Marci asked.

He looked at her and nodded. "Right. I said I wouldn't shoot anybody, and I started to run for the door. That's when he shot me in the shoulder and I went down. Then he grabbed me and tied us together and put that awful tasting muzzle in my mouth. You know the rest."

"You'll testify about all you've told us involving the murder of Henry Rhonstadt?"

"Yes. Nobody should kill a man that way. Osgood is an animal. I don't want him out running around loose."

"You didn't agree to testify simply because you'd get a lesser charge or no charges against you at all?" Spur asked.

"No. I volunteered. Miss Philburton told me maybe I wouldn't be charged later."

"Clare, you don't have to worry about Osgood hurting anyone else. I was chasing him this morning and he died under the wheels of the train."

"Oh, God. Must have been horrible."

"It was quick. Quicker than a hanging." Spur let the young man absorb the idea that Osgood was no longer a threat to anyone. "Clare, is your father Colonel Duncan Franks?"

Clare looked up, amazement washing over his face. "Yeah, but how did you know? I ain't told nobody about that."

"I rode with your father on one campaign. The big one just before he got wounded. I understand you want to be a writer."

"Yeah, like Mark Twain. I love to read his writing."

"Are you as good as he is?" Marci asked.

Clare chuckled. "Course not. Not yet, at least. Maybe I can get good like him after I do it awhile."

"If you go to prison, Clare, what would you do?"

"Try to find a place I could work and write at the same time. I don't know if I could do that."

"If you don't go to prison, what would you do?" Marci asked.

"Know that for sure. I'd head back to the farm and work half time at the farm and do my writing half time. I think Pa would allow that. After all, I'm twenty-one. Should be able to call my shots."

"What about the counterfeiting and the robbery?" Spur asked. "You know you broke the law both times. It was a criminal conspiracy to plan the train robbery. Then depositing counterfeit money with the intent to defraud a banker, that's grand larceny. Most judges would give you ten years for that."

"Ten years! Oh, God, what have I done?"

"That could put off your writing career considerably."

Clare slumped on the chair and held his head in his hands. "What have I done to myself?"

The next afternoon the three of them arrived at Langtry, Texas. Marci and Spur marched up to pay their respects to Judge Roy Bean. Clare said he'd hunt up a buggy.

Judge Roy Bean looked at their credentials and snorted.

"Be damned. Ain't never seen no Treasury

Agent before. Don't think I ever even heard tell of no Secret Service. But if'n you say it's so, I guess should be." They sat in two chairs near a desk that served as the judge's bench. He motioned to the other side of the 20 foot room.

"Come on over to my saloon and let me set up a drink for the both of you. Sarsaparilla for the lady, and a whiskey for the gent."

Spur saw the picture of the English actress and motioned to it. "I see you're quite taken with Lily Langtry."

"He did it!" Somebody at a table bellowed. "You said the precious name of the lady and now you are bound by tradition to set up whiskey for everyone in the house. Including this lady."

Spur looked at the judge who had slid behind a narrow bar and set eight whiskey glasses on the counter and filled them.

"That's the tradition, son. Be eight dollars, Government Man. Only proper we drink to the great Lily Langtry with the best Tennessee sipping whiskey that money can buy. That's a dollar a shot." He held out his hand. Spur tossed him a gold eagle and held out his hand for the two dollars in change. It came back in paper notes. Spur looked at them carefully, passed them to Marci who made a great act of inspecting them for flaws. At last she nodded.

The judge had been holding his breath, now he let it out. The others came rushing to the bar to claim their free drinks.

They all lifted their glasses and looked at Marci.

"A toast to the greatest actress and most beautiful woman in the world, Lily Langtry," Judge Roy Bean brayed. The men tipped the shot glasses and drained them, then looked at Marci. She lifted her brows, then the glass, and in one huge gulp downed the fiery liquid. She coughed twice, her eyes watered and then she laughed.

"This is one day I'll never forget," she said.

Spur turned to the judge. "You know Colonel Franks?"

"Hell, yes. Been around here most as long as I have."

"His spread any good?"

"Will be, soon as he gets some more good brood stock."

"What about his son, Clarence?"

"Boy lost his mother two years or so ago. Wants to be a writer. Comes in here now and then. Seems like a nice boy. Never had any trouble with him."

Spur nodded. "Oh, Judge. You remember that Railway Express car robbery here a few weeks back?"

"Certainly."

"One of the items missing from the registered mail was the front and back engravings for the twenty-dollar United States Treasury Note. The government was considerably upset. Just wanted to report to you that the robbery has been solved. One of the two robbers was shot dead in San Antonio three days ago. The engraving plates and almost all of the counterfeit notes have been recovered. Thought you might want to put that in your court records somewhere."

"Yes, yes. Anyone I know?"

"One of the robbers was Henry Rhonstadt. He had visited your saloon here from time to time. The other robber headed west and hasn't been heard from."

"Rhonstadt. Yes, not much of a Western man, I'm afraid. A transplanted easterner."

Spur agreed and stood along with Marci. She caught his sleeve as she came upright.

"Been interesting meeting you, Judge. Take care of things until we come back."

"Do that, do that. Got me a court case coming up in the morning. Hanging offense, might go easy on the lad." He waved and moved down the short bar to pour a man a beer.

Outside they went to the dozen shacklike buildings that lined the tracks and found Clare had rented the only buggy in town.

"You don't have to come out and see my father," Clare said.

"Oh, but we do," Spur said. "I'm putting you in his custody and I want regular reports. He has to agree to it."

An hour later around the big claw footed table in the parlor, Spur told the rancher about the donnybrook centered around the counterfeit money.

Colonel Franks had sat stiff backed throughout the recital. He looked at his son. "Clarence, what do you have to say in your defense?"

Spur shook his head and stood. "No, Colonel. This isn't a military court martial. Miss Philburton and I have total authority here. We've decided not to prosecute since Clare has volunteered to testify for the prosecution.

"What we want to be certain of is that he spends at least half of his time here at the ranch working on his writing, his stories, his manuscripts. We want your assurance that he'll be required to put in that much time on his muse."

"Oh," Colonel Franks relaxed a little, nodded.

"I see. That puts an entirely different slant on the matter. For the good of the service and that sort of thing. Yes, I understand. A man can't waste ten years in the stockade and be expected to amount to much. Yes, good planning." He looked at Clare. "You heard your sentence. I hope you're prepared to carry out the required work."

"I am, father."

"Well, so. All right. I accept the duty of guard house lout to be sure he serves his sentence."

Spur grinned. "That about takes care of our business. Oh, I do have one textbook for Clare to work with." Spur brought out a book from a small kit he carried and handed the volume to Clare. Spur had scoured San Antonio until he found it the night before they left.

"The works of Mark Twain," Clare read. "Wonderful!" he jumped up and hugged Marci and shook hands with Spur.

"I don't know how I can thank you for what you've done for me."

Spur shrugged. "Make us proud of you. I'll be watching the papers and the magazines and the book stores to see your byline on something one of these days. Work at it. Samuel Clemens did a lot of writing before he sold much."

"Who?" Colonel Franks asked.

"Mark Twain," Clare said. "His real name is Samuel Clemens."

Just before dusk the east bound train came through and stopped at Langtry, Texas. Spur talked with the conductor for a few minutes and then escorted Marci on board. The train was part work train with freight cars and three passenger cars. The road men called it a "mixed" train.

Spur carried their luggage through one passenger car and nudged Marci into the next one. She turned with delight.

"Spur, a sleeper car, a pullman!"

They had tickets straight through to New Orleans, and the conductor promised them that they wouldn't have to change cars until they got to the Louisiana city.

"We can wire our chiefs from Houston," Marci said. "Let them know that the case is wrapped up. I'll have to go back to Washington, I'm sure. But we should be able to stall them a couple of days in New Orleans."

Spur grinned. They sat in the pullman seats until the porter came to make up their beds. Marci had the lower and Spur the top one.

Two hours later when it was dark outside, Marci discovered what had eluded her all these years. She grinned up at Spur where they lay on the bottom bunk.

"Lordy, lordy, lordy. A body can make love in a pullman bunk. It's a bit crowded, but that just lends a note of the bizarre to the affair."

Spur grinned and kissed her again. He wasn't thinking about law breakers. He wasn't thinking about where his next assignment might take him. For the next two days he was out of touch with the world and touching someone special and kind and loving and amazing. Something poked him in the ribs.

"Again?" he said.

Marci giggled. "Yes, again. We can't waste time, We'll only be in this glorious little cocoon of ours until we get to New Orleans."

A few minutes later, Spur didn't quite hear what

she said. He bent closer. Marci giggled and told him again.

"You want to be on top? Damn, now that's going to take some doing."

"We have two days to figure it out," Marci said, and they both chuckled.

**DIRK FLETCHER**

**A double blast of hard cases and hussies for one low price!**
**A $7.98 value for only $4.99!**

***Bodie Beauties.*** Fighting alone against a vicious band of crooks, Spur receives unexpected help from a lovely lady of the evening. If Jessica doesn't wear Spur out, he'll put the crooks away forever.
*And in the same pistol-hot edition...*
***Frisco Foxes.*** While taking the die for a gold coin to the San Francisco mint, McCoy has to fight off thieving bastards who want to get their greedy hands on the dies, and bodacious beauties who want Spur's loving hands all over them.
_3486-7 BODIE BEAUTIES/FRISCO FOXES (two books in one) only $4.99

***Kansas City Chorine.*** While trying to catch a vicious killer, Spur tangles with a pompous preacher who is fleecing his innocent flock and a blonde chorus girl who is determined to skin him alive.
*And in the same exciting volume...*
***Plains Paramour.*** Spur is assigned to hunt down a murderous hangman in Quintoch, Kansas. But a sexy suffragette with some liberated ideas keeps him so tied up in the bedroom he has little strength left to wrap up the case.
_3544-8 KANSAS CITY CHORINE/PLAINS PARAMOUR (two books in one) only $4.99

**LEISURE BOOKS**
**ATTN: Order Department**
**276 5th Avenue, New York, NY 10001**

Please add $1.50 for shipping and handling for the first book and $.35 for each book thereafter. PA., N.Y.S. and N.Y.C. residents, please add appropriate sales tax. No cash, stamps, or C.O.D.s. All orders shipped within 6 weeks via postal service book rate. Canadian orders require $2.00 extra postage and must be paid in U.S. dollars through a U.S. banking facility.

Name ______________________________
Address ______________________________
City ____________________ State ______ Zip ______
I have enclosed $______ in payment for the checked book(s).
Payment must accompany all orders. ☐ Please send a free catalog.

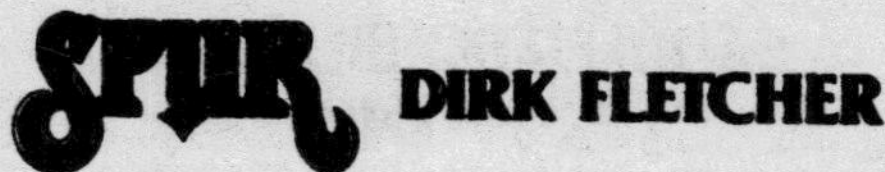


**The pistol-hot Western series filled with more brawls and beauties than a frontier saloon on a Saturday night!**

*Spur #40: Texas Tramp.* When a band of bloodthirsty Comanches kidnaps the sultry daughter of a state senator, the sheriff of Sweet Springs call on Spur McCoy to rescue the tempting Penny Wallington. Once McCoy chops the Indians' totem poles down to size, he will have Penny for his thoughts—and a whole lot of woman in his hands.
_3523-5 $3.99 US/$4.99 CAN

*Spur #39: Minetown Mistress.* While tracking down a missing colonel in Idaho Territory, Spur runs into a luscious blonde and a randy redhead who appoint themselves his personal greeters. He'll waste no time finding the lost man—because only then can he take a ride with the fillies who drive his private welcome wagon.
_3448-4 $3.99 US/$4.99 CAN

*Spur #38: Free Press Filly.* Sent to investigate the murder of a small-town newspaper editor, McCoy is surprised to discover his contact is Gypsy, the man's busty daughter, who believes in a free press and free love. Gun's blazing, lust raging, McCoy has to kill the killer so he can put the story—and Gypsy—to bed.
_3394-1 $3.99 US/$4.99 CAN

**LEISURE BOOKS**
**ATTN: Order Department**
**276 5th Avenue, New York, NY 10001**

Please add $1.50 for shipping and handling for the first book and $.35 for each book thereafter. PA., N.Y.S. and N.Y.C. residents, please add appropriate sales tax. No cash, stamps, or C.O.D.s. All orders shipped within 6 weeks via postal service book rate. Canadian orders require $2.00 extra postage and must be paid in U.S. dollars through a U.S. banking facility.

Name ______________________________________________
Address ____________________________________________
City ______________________________ State ______ Zip ______
I have enclosed $______in payment for the checked book(s).
Payment must accompany all orders. ☐ Please send a free catalog.

# SADDLER DOUBLE EDITION

## Gene Curry

## TWICE THE FILLIES! TWICE THE FIGHTS! TWO COMPLETE ADULT WESTERNS IN ONE DOUBLE EDITION!

***A Dirty Way To Die.*** After a big win in a poker game, Saddler treats himself to the tastiest tart in a fancy New Orlean's brothel. Then he finds himself wanted for the murder of the cathouse madam. But Saddler won't run—he'll stand up to the bastards and shoot until his six-gun is spent.

*And in the same pistol-hot volume...*

***Colorado Crossing.*** Liz Kelley is an ornery hellcat with a price on her head. Saddler's willing to bring her back to her father and collect a hefty reward, but her desperado boyfriend has other ideas. Soon Saddler has the outlaw hot to send him to Boot Hill and the wildcat heiress itching to gun him down—between the sheets or anywhere else.

__3576-6 **(2 books in one volume)** $4.99

***Ace In The Hole.*** When Saddler finds himself riding and robbing with the infamous Butch Cassidy, things get real hot real fast: The ladies want his hide, the lawmen want his head, and one ornery hombre won't rest until he's dead.

*And in the same action-packed volume...*

***Yukon Ride.*** Sent to the icy Yukon to transport Judge Phineas Slocum's body to San Francisco, Saddler thinks his journey through the frozen region will be hell—until he meets some wanton angels who are anything but frigid. But life is cheap in the frozen North, and if Saddler isn't careful, he'll end up as dead as Phineas Slocum.

__3750-5 **(2 books in one volume)** $4.99 US/$5.99 CAN

**Dorchester Publishing Co., Inc.**
**65 Commerce Road**
**Stamford, CT 06902**

Please add $1.75 for shipping and handling for the first book and $.50 for each book thereafter. NY, NYC, PA and CT residents, please add appropriate sales tax. No cash, stamps, or C.O.D.s. All orders shipped within 6 weeks via postal service book rate. Canadian orders require $2.00 extra postage and must be paid in U.S. dollars through a U.S. banking facility.

Name ____________________

Address ____________________

City ____________________ State ______ Zip ______

I have enclosed $______ in payment for the checked book(s).

Payment must accompany all orders. ☐ Please send a free catalog.